# BLOODLINES

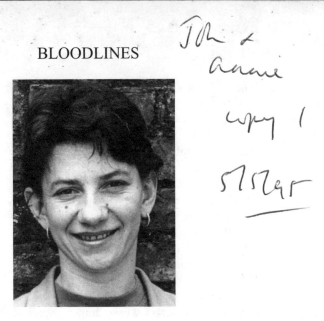

*Jhn &
Anne

copy 1

5/5/95*

Julia Darling was born in 1956 in Winchester, in the house that Jane Austen died in.

After a turbulent education at various schools, she trained as a Cordon Bleu Chef before studying Fine Art at Falmouth in Cornwall.

In 1980 she moved to Newcastle upon Tyne, and worked in Sunderland as an arts worker for some years. Then she had two daughters and gave up a regular wage to concentrate on writing, which she has been doing since 1987.

In 1994 she spent three months writing her first novel in Western Australia.

She now, lives in Heaton in Newcastle, trying to tame a steep unruly garden. She has no cats.

D0530750

The writer wishes to acknowledge the following magazines and publishers, in which some stories have appeared.
Stand Magazine
Writing Women
Imago (Australian National New Fiction)
The Western Review (Australia)
Littlewood Arc
Northern Stories
A19 Film and Video, Sunderland who commissioned two stories.
The Women's Press
The Page
Westerly (Australia)
Panurge

Thanks to Liz Atkin whose drawing sparked the story *Pearl* and also to Pat Fisher for inspiration. Also thanks to Charlie Hardwick, Jane Barnett and Karin Young.

# BLOODLINES

*Julia Darling*

PANURgE
PUBLISHING

Brampton, Cumbria
1995

# BLOODLINES by JULIA DARLING

first published 1995 by
Panurge Publishing
Crooked Holme Farm Cottage
Brampton, Cumbria CA8 2AT

EDITOR  John Murray
PRODUCTION EDITOR  Henry Swan
COVER DESIGN  Andy Williams

Typeset at Union Lane Telecentre, Brampton, Cumbria CA8 1BX
Tel. 016977 - 41014
Printed by Peterson's, 12 Laygate, South Shields, Tyne and Wear  NE33 5RP
Tel. 0191-456-3493

ISBN 1 898984 25 5

Copyright JULIA DARLING 1995

British Library Cataloguing in Publication Data.
A catalogue record for this book is available from
the British Library.

PANURGE PUBLISHING
Crooked Holme Farm Cottage,
Brampton,
Cumbria  CA8 2AT
Tel.  016977-41087

*for Bev, Scarlet and Florrie*

# BLOODLINES

# Bloodlines

The letters are all blue and flimsy. Airmail is so unsatisfactory. Not like vellum. Sometimes I don't even open them when they arrive. I just put them straight into the carrier bag behind the stereo. The writing is always the same, and they inevitably begin with - "I hope you are well."

Sometimes I am not well. Sometimes I have been dreaming about savage dogs, or pavements with cracks in them. There are days when I find this city quite alarming and can't bear to look at it. It's full of leaking arcades that have been dampened by foul outbursts of rain, and car parks that loom up when you least expect them, and shops with huge cavernous mouths that pull you in. On such days I generally stay in bed and try to write letters back to my father in Madrid.

He would like me to go and see him, but I am uncomfortable with my father. He is too big. He cuts the light out of rooms. I remember his loud voice making me jump when I was a baby, or I think I do. My mother won't speak of him at all since the divorce. She has married an interior decorator called Paul, and lives in Hertfordshire.

My father writes and tells me that he will pay my fare, with his golden card with the eagle flying across it, and that he has a spare room and a housekeeper called Rosa.

The first time I read about the housekeeper I was on the train going home. I live at the end of the line and every day I step neatly onto the buzzing yellow train that sweeps into the morose station where I live. Candycoats, Hawkersville, Mankerton, Subside Village, Overflank, Middleclaw, Wegsfield, Fallows Yard, and then Barberstown, which is the centre, where I limp out, like a mole burrowing out into a builder's yard. After five minutes I am blasted with dust particles and nearly flattened by women with large bags.

I started reading about the housekeeper as we drew into Subside. It was the first interesting thing my father had told me in five years of correspondence. He said, dryly, that she was an excellent, if uneducated housekeeper, apart from during the full moon when she changed dramatically and he had been forced to lock his drinks cabinet.

I laughed. It was the thought of my father; large, English and unshiftable, being prey to the unstable cycles of a Spanish country woman. I was sure she drank red wine.

I work for the Dock Refurbishment Council on a temporary contract. Coincidentally I often call in sick, due to my own monthly cyclical problems. I heave and weep and generally swell.

At the moment we are building a great embossed tower in the middle of a mosaic paved square. It will glitter in bright sunlight.

The aim is to attract visitors to this rather infertile city. I phone people up and describe the tower in great detail. I talk to strangers as if they are my oldest friends. We're launching the tower like a space rocket on the night of the Summer Solstice, and there will be a dazzling firework display with rockets, and even the head of a Northern man drinking a pint of beer illuminated across the rotting harbour.

I am very attached to the tower. Sometimes I feel it belongs to me, in all its ridiculousness. I am familiar with every part of its making; its inner rubble, its window measurements, and even the number of tiny glass mirrors pressed into its Gaudiesque body.

It is the work of an architect from Brazil. I like to think of how much it has cost the government. I like to watch it growing from blue lines on paper into this solid edifice. It will always be there. Even when I am old.

Publicly I am the woman in a small suit who rustles behind joking business men with a file full of coloured paper. Sometimes they turn to me and place their big palms across my back in a leaning, almost caring way. How I got into this kind of employment beats me. I was Head Girl at school, maybe that's the root of it.

I will also tell you that since those heady days at Walthamstow Girl's Grammar, I have always been attracted to other girls. I'm a dyke, a lemon, a lesbo, a queer. Perhaps that's why I am uncomfortable with my father.

Like most people I know, my love life is a series of incomplete disasters. Unlike them, I do not have fantasies about the right person, and I have never advertised in the Guardian Lonely Hearts Column, or contacted a dating agency. I prefer the condition of lovelessness, to be honest. I am at home with it.

When the letter came about the housekeeper I was single, but soon after that the wine bar opened on the river bank, and I met Sandra Diaz.

I went to the wine bar after work in order to fortify myself for the long shuttle home. Da Vinci's reminded me of my father, sat in his Spanish hat waiting for his housekeeper to appear with an omelette, or a flagon of Sangria. It was a superficial connection - strings of onions and raffia-coated bottles. The pictures of bulls reminded me of him particularly.

The Dock Refurbishment Council had invited artists from European countries to create public works to coincide with the launching of the great tower. Although I wasn't in charge of that particular set of files and complicated phone numbers, having no linguistic skill, and no knowledge of modern art, I did realise that the woman in reflective sunglasses was probably foreign, and probably artistic. She drank Newcastle Brown with interest, and kept looking at the ceiling. Also she smoked Parisiennes, which stank of the French underground and foreign ashtrays.

I was mid-cycle, so my sense of smell was heightened.

Then Gordon came in from Artworks which is the department next to ours in a prefabricated hut, and said hallo to me and Sandra simultaneously, so I had to sit down and join in the fragmented conversation. I wasn't surprised when she said she came from Madrid; after all, one thing follows another. Once you start thinking about omelettes, or babies, or dogs, they seem to be everywhere. They even come out of the radio as you think about them. That night it was Learn Spanish on Radio Four, and the day before I had been to Safeways and every tin I put in the trolley turned out to be of Spanish origin.

The minute I saw Sandra I knew she was loose. She was the kind of woman who just floats into situations, acting alarmed, but is in fact entirely at ease with the oddest liaison. She had very short, Spanish blonde hair and a defined forehead. She made en-crusted textiles, she said, and had work hanging in the Museum Of Modern Art.

"So what," I thought. The stink of her Parisiennes was getting me down. I felt a sick note coming on. Gordon slavered all over her anyway. He talked about Art the way other people talk about meals; as if he consumed it daily.

In order to change the course of the conversation that was centring on an airtight fishtank, with sonic tapes booming over-head, I mentioned to Sandra that my father lived in Madrid, and she looked at me as if I was accusing her of something.

"What does he do, this father of yours?" she said.

"He's a linguist, and who knows what they get up to."

Then, with a slight sense of disloyalty, I told her over the next half hour about the housekeeper and the fits she had during men-struation. Since the first letter my father had written again, de-scribing a drinks party with colleagues from the Institute of Latin

Studies.

Things had been quite unexceptional at first, with Rosa bringing trays of cocktails onto the balcony, demurely and subserviently. Then, gradually, she had gone downhill, and started to stagger. Finally, like some Grace Pool lookalike she had fallen onto the floor, clutching her matted head and moaning.

My father hadn't sacked her, although he said he had been stern, but "the poor woman is in the throes of the moon, and seems to have no will of her own at certain times."

I thought the story quite amusing, but Sandra whistled through her white teeth and shook her head. Then she took off her sunglasses, exposing black diamond eyes. Sandra reached over the straw beermats and grasped my wrist.

"Country women are very suspicious."

I think she meant superstitious, but I was looking at her slim brown hands and feeling a bit shaky. Nothing had touched me apart from the palms of business men for nearly three years. Her touch had the smell of some exotic French brandy, or bay leaf, or eucalyptus.

Gordon coughed and left, though we hardly noticed him.

In the end we tottered back to the underground together and slid down the escalator at Barberstown, singing the Internationale. By Middleclaw we were holding hands, and by the time we touched Hawkersville her tongue was behind my ear. Luckily she looked like a boy in her anonymous shades, or we might have regretted our actions at Candycoats, when an inspector had to shake us apart, like dogs, to tell us that the train terminated here.

The only other thing I remember about that night is that it was a crescent moon and for a while we lay in the back garden looking up at it surrounded by nettles, which miraculously didn't sting me.

The next day, while red wine still coursed through my throbbing veins, a letter arrived from my father, saying that Rosa was much improved and had just made an excellent paella, having apologised profusely for her behaviour.

The summer continued with raw passion and modern art intertwined, like my and Sandra's legs as we rolled about, always with a bottle of some cheap wine half-empty by the bed. I wonder now how I ever got to work at all, but somehow the beautiful phallic tower continued to be built, and the mosaic artists stuck their little golden bits all over it and Sandra made her indecipherable artworks of strewn grass and mud, and I wrote to my father and he wrote back.

I remember one day quite vividly.

Sandra and I took an unopened letter from my father down to the new business park, which was like a neat shanty town with its empty blocks of dusty offices and half finished sculptures. The river was very oily and smelly, and I saw a rose floating down slowly amongst a mass of other debris. We sat on a deserted promenade and opened the letter.

*I hope you are well. I have some excellent news. Perhaps I didn't explain to you that I have been ill with a virus for some weeks* (he had, but my father always tells me everything several times). *Rosa has been looking after me. I don't know what I would have done without her. She is much better generally and her appearance is quite lovely, and as far as I know she no longer drinks and her other problems are much abated.*

The rose was nearly out of sight now, and Sandra didn't seem to be listening.

*The upshot of all this is that I have proposed to Rosa and we are to be married next month. I feel that we can be companions to one another in our old age. It will be a small wedding. Of course I would be delighted if you would like to come over, but I understand this may be difficult for you*

From where we were sitting the mosaic tower glinted maliciously. I felt slightly disturbed by the news of my father's wedding. It suddenly occurred to me that since my passion had been roused my menstrual cycle had been considerably quietened. Then I thought about my father in bed with his dark, superstitious housekeeper and felt uncomfortable.

Sandra took the letter and deftly folded it into a small blue paper boat and dropped it down into the water.

It sailed off.

"Good luck, Daddy," she said morbidly, and I suddenly wanted to be alone, on my way home, on the shunting train. Going back to the end of the line.

As we walked back I was stung by several nettles that the corporation gardeners had left behind.

The next week it was the great launch, and everyone at work became quite frantic with bits of paper flying in all directions. There were a lot of arms on shoulders and heads on desks and tears in the toilet. I had pre-menstrual tension and avoided Sandra. She kept on phoning up with her insistent Spanish voice, which irritated me beyond belief. I wrote to my father, congratulating him on his engagement. I sent him a postcard of the tower ablaze with light.

When the day of the launch finally came I put on a maroon suit and stuffed my shoulder bag with sanitary protection, as my lower abdomen was dark and heavy, like before a storm, and my breasts were concrete balloons. I was just about to leave the house when the phone rang. Of course it was Sandra, who I was beginning to wish I had never met. I could smell her Parisiennes down the phone and the stale pong of her clothes.

Sandra was wailing.

"Oh, for God's sake!" I said curtly.

Then she stopped her wretched braying and whispered nastily:

"I curse you then."

Actually, I breathed a sigh of relief when she said that. All I was thinking about was the colour of my shoes and if they really matched my maroon suit.

"Fair enough!" I quipped, and put the phone down.

On the way to work I counted women who smiled. There were two. One was in her demented eighties, and the other was a pre-pubescent schoolgirl who looked out of the window grinning. The rest were miserable as Christmas.

As soon as I got to the quayside I knew something was wrong. I saw Gordon through his pre-fabricated window, pacing up and down with a mobile phone pinned to his ear. Then I saw the tower. It was splattered with red paint, running into the gullies of its sparkling golden sides. There was a crowd of people gazing at it and shaking their heads. I looked across the square and could have sworn I saw Sandra, glowering ferociously in the shadows.

I started to run towards her, my stupid shoes twisting on the cobbles, but she was gone. There seemed to be paper blowing everywhere; reports and clip files, and transparent paper holders, and memos. I was hot with rage. I felt as if I was foaming at the mouth; trapped, blown and uncontrolled.

Then Gordon grabbed my arm. He looked oddly calm amongst the wreckage. I looked at him bluntly.

"There's a phone call for you," he stated. "From Madrid."

I got a sudden whiff of *tapas* when he said that, and felt immediately nauseous.

Gordon had turned. I was supposed to follow him. I hobbled back to the office. All around me police and passers-by were muttering. It began to rain, suddenly and intensely, and as I walked to the phone I saw that the water was washing away some of the paint, and red puddles were appearing on the ground.

"It's only acrylic," Gordon was saying, conversationally.

I picked up the receiver and spoke dumbly into it.

"Yes."

It was a thick, Spanish voice. A woman. She seemed to be crying but it was hard to know the difference between the sound of the rain and her voice.

"Your father. He has a heart attack. He has passed on."

I suddenly thought it was Sandra, playing some ghastly trick.

"Who is this?" I said angrily.

"Rosa." Then I realised how her voice slurred and that she was drunk.

"What do you mean, passed on?"

Then there was a loud noise; a clap of lightning or something and I dropped the phone. I'm not sure what happened after that. I think I was sick.

I am at home now. I'm lying in bed and bleeding. None of the fireworks would light, so the day was a wash-out, and there will be no tourists flooding to see the pinkish tower. My contract is ended.

Tomorrow I will fly to Madrid and sort out the funeral. I can't imagine my father in a coffin. He will never fit. I can't stop thinking of unspiritual things.

And I wish Sandra would come, and stroke my head and help me drink a bottle of red wine, but I am completely alone, here at the end of the line.

The last letter from my father was a boat; a blue boat, sailing off down a river. It will have disintegrated by now.

And there will be no more letters.

I lie here with the carrier bag emptied over the mattress, under a sea of thin, blue paper.

# *Pearl*

Pearl has two faces. When she is standing on the crossing holding her lollipop stick she has a buttery smile and eyes that slant upwards. After the cars have gone she turns and her dark face with the pursed mouth and the two lines on her forehead, crosses her features, like a stage curtain.

Lollipop ladies never have uniforms that fit. They always look lonely. I think of Pearl like that; as a round shape in a square world. I dream about her sometimes. Embarrassing dreams about swimming and world wars. She is in them, changing faces like the weather.

Perhaps it is the knitting.

When Pearl isn't being a lollipop lady she sits on a wall by the crossing and knits. Once I read in a newspaper about a woman who was banned from a public house for knitting in the corner. The male customers said it disturbed them. She took the manager to court and won, so I suppose the men went somewhere else. It's very hard to get to know someone who always knits, and you never know what they're thinking when they're clicking away.

I walk over the crossing every day. The walk is so boring that I can't even remember doing it some days. There is a chemist's shop, and a row of pruned trees, then the crossing, then the footpath through a dismal trodden-down park to the school gate. I see the same people each morning and afternoon, mothers mostly; barging along with prams, muttering, hunching their shoulders in the wind. I don't know what they do the rest of the time. These people are stuck in my memory trudging along the pavement. We say things to each other like:

"Are we late?"

18

or

"Christ it's cold!"

I am eight months pregnant. I am dreaming most of the time. Things are very slow; very methodical. My daughter doesn't like the idea of the baby. She doesn't understand how it happened.She says it will smell. She wants me to have it adopted. I am sure that she will come round when the baby is born. We are very close.

One muddy morning we get to the crossing and Pearl says:

"Not long now!" and I sigh appropriately.

Then she rummages about in her plastic coat and pulls out something wrapped in tissue paper. Something soft.

"Open it," says Pearl with her good face.

"Yes, open it," says my daughter.

It is a pair of booties with little pink ribbons threaded through them. They smell of cigarettes. My daughter is enchanted. I thank Pearl twice and wander on. I can feel Pearl watching me. I'm not sure if I behaved properly.

I don't know why, but it becomes more of an ordeal crossing the road after that. I feel I have to say something grateful. I search for pleasantries. Another mother tells me that Pearl always knits things for other people's babies.

"Isn't she kind," says the other mother.

"Oh yes," I agree. She is.

A week later Pearl gives me another package. This time it's a matinee jacket with mother of pearl buttons. It's tiny; it would fit one of my daughter's dolls. I am, of course, doubly grateful, even though I'm not all that keen on traditional baby clothes in white, pink or blue. I like to dress my babies in yellow or red.

At home I lay out the new babies things on the floor in neat piles. I have bought some expensive soap, and a huge bra like a harness with fat straps. I have a pair of man's pyjamas to wear after the birth. I have sewn up the the front. I put Pearl's presents on one side. I don't really want them.

I wonder if Pearl is curious about the father. I got the sperm through a self-help group. I administered it with a cake-icing syringe. I was incredulous when it worked. It felt like an immaculate conception. I have tried to explain it to my daughter but she looks suspicious. She's taken to talking about storks.

A week before I am due to go into labour Pearl gives me a third parcel. I open it in the rain. It is a hat with a bobble hanging from the top and two ear flaps. It must have been very difficult to knit. I thank her again, but perhaps she senses a weariness in my voice, because her dark face crosses her features like a cloud passing, and I shudder. Late pregnancy is a really peculiar state. I am so over-sensitive that anything can make me feel like crying. The hat has that effect on me. I throw it into the nearest rubbish bin and walk on guiltily.

That night my contractions start. They are like cart-horses galloping through my body. I am having a home birth. My friends loom over me with sponges and ice. The midwife has to fight her way through cheering lesbians to deliver my baby.

He is born at dawn. He cries like a blackbird. My daughter looks at her brother clutching a baby doll. The doll is wearing Pearl's knitted clothes, just like a real baby.

Afterwards I fall asleep; hearing distant jubilation and champagne bubbling in the kitchen.

A fortnight later I am walking to school again, pushing the baby in a large and ornate pram I bought at an Oxfam shop. I am very proud of it. It has silver fittings and a navy blue canopy with tassels. The baby looks angelic, with smooth skin and fingers that curl into tiny crescents. He is wearing a velveteen babygro. Some of the mothers slip silver coins under the baby's rug. It is a custom round here. I nod beatifically and push on, feeling light and proud of myself. When I see Pearl she has a dark brooding expression, and I suddenly recall the hat. I smile at her hopefully. She looms over the precipice of the pram edge.

Before I even speak Pearl has picked up the baby. There is a crowd of women flapping like crows around me, watching. Pearl squeezes the baby into her coarse plastic coat and glowers. I am suddenly  frightened. I step towards her. A vast lorry thunders past, splashing my legs with water.

"Give him back Pearl," I say loudly.

All the other mothers are cawing and crowing. I reach out to take the baby, and Pearl shakes her head and steps back.  I am nearly hysterical.

Then a big mother in a mackintosh shouts militaristically:

"PUT THAT BABY DOWN!" and Pearl's face changes and she grins apologetically and puts the baby back in the pram.

"Isn't he a darling!" she says in a quite normal voice.

But the crowd of women are shaking their heads maliciously, and my daughter is crying.

When I get home I phone up the council and register a complaint. They are very soothing.

My friends come round and discuss Pearl at length. I get into bed and leave them to it. I feel obscurely guilty. I don't mention the hat.


Pearl disappears.

There is a new red-haired lollipop lady who doesn't knit and who wears wellington boots. She looks homely and rural.

As the months go by I look for Pearl. Sometimes I think I see her sad large shape passing my window, or at the far end of supermarkets. I don't forget her. She is still in my dreams.

The baby sits up now, and pummels his fists on the floor.  My daughter plays with him. Her doll still wears the white bootees and the matinee jacket, although they are dirty and the wool is unravelling in some places.

One day she comes home from school with a face that is soggy with unwiped tears. When I try to comfort her she pushes me away.

"What is it?" I say, trying to be kind.

"Other kids," she says, holding her doll as if she wants to strangle it.

"What about them?"

"They said you were a pervert."

Of course it was bound to happen. I search them out with my eyes on the way to school and curse them.

My daughter makes me wear a dress and lipstick. I feel as if I am acting.

Increasingly, after that, I feel isolated on the walk to school, as if there is a subtle silence in the air. I keep my head up and walk quickly.

Months pass.

It is June when Pearl appears, and the walk to school is green and leisurely. The children are all dressed in tee-shirts and shorts and climbing on the walls. I push my baby along in a buggy. He is hot and blotchy. I am beginning to consider the world beyond these small streets.

At first I don't recognise her. She is standing in the park next to a municipal rose bush licking a strawberry ice cream. She is wearing a summer hat and looking undeniably handsome. Her other hand rests on the bar of a spanking new pram.

At first I turn the other way, thinking that I will make a detour around the sandpit to avoid colliding with her on the narrow path, then my daughter says loudly:

"There's Pearl," and she looks up and sees us.

She waves.

I am very embarrassed then, even afraid of her, but I walk towards her, driven by curiosity.

As we get nearer she gives a proud, royal nod, and I smile bravely, suddenly remembering that I should slip a silver coin into the pram for a new baby.

"Hallo Pearl," I say conversationally, gripping a fifty pence piece in my hand.

My son giggles and points at Pearl's hat.

"He's grown," she says, her face a crease of smiles.

I lean over the pram indulgently, and pull back the cotton sheet.

The first thing I see is a white knitted hat with earflaps, neatly tied around a small head. I lean in further.

"What's its name?" asks my daughter.

Pearl pauses, then says, "It's a she."

I see the baby's face then. It is small and perfect, beautifully crafted in skin-coloured wool.

Pearl has knitted herself a baby.

My mouth hangs open. I struggle for words, but she has turned on her heels and is walking across the park, away from me, disappearing into a leafy avenue of trees, like a spell.

# Nesting

Gabrielle told me that she met Hilary in a beech wood behind the motorway. She was alone, crumbling bread up in her pockets and dropping it, hoping no one would see her. It was a light, dry day, and she said the leaves crunched like Cornflakes under her shoes. It was frosty.

Gabrielle always describes things this way, as if they were edible.

Then she said, she heard a voice, calling her.

Gabrielle was thirteen then, an unlucky age.

At the time I felt powerless, inadequate, and angry.

Our doctor, a great bulbous woman with greasy pores, would lecture me and Gabrielle as we sat before her, speechless.

She said that anorexia was like suicide, and that there would come a point from which Gabrielle could not return. I must make Gabrielle believe that she was worth saving, but the doctor didn't seem to know how. She had labradors, not children.

I even phoned up an expert in California, who was reputed to have saved many girls. She said:

"Honey, why can't you just put your arms around her and tell her that you love her, and that you'll never leave her," and I put the phone down, because I am a working mother, and the Californian's voice was sugary and over-rich, and I had the feeling she was blaming me too.

I had Gabrielle when I was sixteen. I got pregnant with an amorous boy scout who was younger than me. I didn't realise boy scouts were capable of fatherhood. I don't think he did either. Neither of us was aware of the resilient seed that must have found its way through my regulation knickers to my ovaries, a hundred yards from a camp fire, in a fumble of shorts and straps, while the rest of the troop sung 'She'll Be Coming Round The Mountain'.

My mother prayed for months, as I swelled. I got tired of being forgiven. She is very devout.

After two years of living at home in a state of perpetual shame I moved into a council flat. Mother said I was moving in with Satan, but actually I was quite alone.

I trained as a beautician. She said that was wicked too. The house I grew up in was beige and ordinary, with chipped mugs on hooks in the kitchen and pale nylon covers from charity shops on the beds. I have always wanted beauty. My own daughter has dry blotchy skin. That's another failure.

To goad my mother I sometimes date a British Telecom engineer called Gary, but I only fancy him when he's up a ladder. I got a job on a skin counter in a department store, and I was due for promotion.

Then Gabrielle became anorexic, and mother nodded and smirked as if Satan had been there all along, hiding in the fridge.

Perhaps he has.

Perhaps he is in me.

Sometimes I want to shake Gabrielle. Other times I am kind and make her small tasty meals that I try and feed her with a spoon. I was at the end of my recipe book when Gabrielle met Hilary. That's why I went along with it. I would have believed anything.

She came home happy after her walk in the beech wood, and told me that she had met a woman who lived up a tree.

"Really," I said. "Eat a boiled egg."

But Gabrielle didn't answer. She sat down at the kitchen table and looked at me as if I was her jailer. She said:

"I like being up in the air. Like a saint."

"Look," I said, "you'll have to go back into hospital if you go on like that."

This is a conversation we have all the time.

It gets tedious.

Then she ate some boiled egg.

"I looked up and there she was."

"Who?"

"Hilary."

"Why is she living up a tree?"

"She says that living on the ground is too difficult."

The next day I went to work. I had a woman come in with bags under her eyes and a shagreen complexion. I spent an hour smoothing it out with a small roller and filling in holes with putty. Eventually she looked ten years younger, although she couldn't shut her eyes. All the time I was worrying about Gabrielle and hoping that she was eating her lunch, not burying it in the garden, or feeding it to the neighbour's poodle.

When I got a break I went straight to the telephone, which staff are only supposed to use for emergencies, and rang home.

My mother answered.

"What the hell are you doing there?" I said, as the supervisor walked past.

"Forgive her Lord," barks my mother. Then, nastily: "You shouldn't be working."

She always goes straight to the needle point in my stomach.

"Where's Gabrielle?" I shouted.

"Out."

The supervisor stood behind me twitching.

"I can't talk now," I snapped.

"I'd better find her for you, hadn't I?"

"She's probably gone to the shops, that's all."

"You know what I think."

"Yes." I slammed the receiver down.

I had to fill in on perfumes all afternoon because of that phone call. I stood there spraying the wrists of poor women who were as likely to buy a bottle of 'Desire' as the Pope.

One woman said to me:

"Smells like fly spray," and tripped off laughing. I sprayed the back of her coat with it, feeling like a tomcat with its hackles up, then met the supervisor's eyes across the shop floor.

Gabrielle and my mother were ruining my career.

'Desire' does smell like fly spray.

On the bus going home I kept thinking about Gabrielle.

I loved her when she was born. She had skin of satin and surprised eyes, and bore no resemblance to a boy scout. I hated it when they wouldn't let me hold her; when I could hear her crying upstairs in a shabby cot, with a gloomy crucifix hanging above her tiny head, while my breasts were leaking milk.

When she was a little girl and we moved to the flat, we had treats all the time. We had chocolate for breakfast and bought clothes from catalogues.

She was quiet, and she was shy, but she had me. I would practise make-up skills on her tiny face, and once she looked in the mirror and started to cry, because she thought I had made her look old, and I had to wipe it all off quickly with babycream.

All the time my mother was coming round trying to save us, and wanting to take Gabrielle back to the old house, but I put my foot down and wouldn't let her.

Gabrielle didn't understand and thought I was being cruel to her Nana. She liked the idea of angels. She liked nativity, and Noah, and even Moses, and the more I cursed these biblical ghosts the more she wanted them. She became pious and sanctimonious, until I felt persecuted by my mother and my daughter, and in the end I gave in, and let Gabrielle go to church with my mother, even though it made me lonely. On Sundays I would go to bed and feel outcast, but then all my life I've felt lonely on Sundays.

The bus lurched into my estate, full of mothers with hairy legs who needed facials, and who rushed away to their hothouse families, faces exposed to the wind. I walked carefully, determined to keep my poise.

At home Gabrielle was alone, sitting at the kitchen table. There was a lemon meringue pie cooking in the oven.

"Where's Nana?" I said.

Gabrielle didn't speak. She shrugged and said:

"You look awful with all that lipstick on."

I rushed to the mirror. I looked miserable, but not awful.

"What's cooking?" I asked, trying to be cheerful.

"I'm making a pie, for Hilary."

"For Hilary?"

Dimly I recalled something the obese doctor had said; that anorexics would do anything to avoid eating, even create fictional people that ate for them. I put my hand on Gabrielle's arm.

"Why don't we have some pie?" I said gently.

"I've already eaten," she said.

"Oh yes, what?"

"A sandwich."

I went to the breadbin. These days I count everything; even slices of bread, apples in the fruit bowl, eggs in the fridge. Some bread had gone.

"Did you really eat the sandwich?" I looked in the rubbish bin. It was empty.

"Of course I ate it. Hilary told me to."

"Is this your friend?"

"Yes. I told you. She lives in a tree."

I wondered if it was too late to phone the doctor, and then

decided I couldn't bear to listen to her voice again, with its pleated vowels and antiseptic morals. I would rather speak to one of her labradors.

"Will you eat something now?" I asked plaintively.

"No, I'm not hungry."

"Did you see Nana?"

"Oh, her." Gabrielle made a face. It cheered me up.

"What did she say?"

"She just went on."

"Oh yeah?"

"On and on. Hilary heard her. We were standing underneath the tree. Hilary dropped a fir cone on her head."

"Did she?" I was warming to Hilary.

"Then what happened?"

"I came home with Nana, and I ate a sandwich."

Gabrielle is not beautiful, but she is startling. She is a small yellow-haired girl with the frail bones of a sparrow. Her eyes are large and brown. It's an unusual combination. I don't know what to do about her. I have never really felt like a proper mother; like the women in supermarkets with children at their heels. She makes me feel clumsy and hard. I weighed her then. She looked so thin standing on the scales that I nearly cried. She had lost half a pound.

I tucked her up in bed that night, and put a glass of milk on her bedside table.

She said, "I'm alright you know. It's alright." I nodded, and stroked her bony head. A strand of hair came off in my hand.

Then she whispered, as if it was a guilty secret:

"Hilary doesn't believe in God," before closing her eyes and turning her face away, so I couldn't answer.

The next morning I heard her getting out of bed at dawn. She went to the kitchen. I staggered in with my red silk dressing-gown on. She was putting an old coat on over her pyjamas.

"What the hell are you doing?" I grunted.

"Going to see Hilary."

She stood there in the new light, holding the pie.

"You can come if you like."

I have not been out of the house with no lipstick on for some years, and I wasn't about to start now. I went back to bed, but couldn't sleep. Birds were coughing in the trees.

I imagined Gabrielle walking through the drowsy estate, with tangled hair and half-closed eyes, carrying a lemon meringue pie. I suddenly thought how madness infects whole households, like a virus. It makes us do all kinds of things. It makes us be the opposite of what we are.

I felt powerless. I wanted to give up.

Gabrielle came back with an empty dish.

"Hilary liked the pie," she said. "I ate some too."

Her fictional friend was turning out to be extremely expensive.

I phoned up work and said I was sick. In a manner of speaking I was. Gabrielle watched television; the light flickering across her face in a room with the curtains drawn. I lay in the bath and smoked.

When my mother called we both hid under the kitchen table.

We heard her marching off down the street huffing and puffing like an old gospel song.

I didn't tell Gabrielle to eat. I opened a tin of baked beans and gobbled them up myself with a spoon. It was a very peaceful, close day. In the evening Gabrielle baked a dark chocolate Devilsfood Cake. I licked out the bowl.

The next morning Gabrielle went out again, carrying the weighty cake in a basket, like Little Red Riding Hood. I didn't stop her. I assumed she was burying it in the wood in some complicated ritual.

Later we had to go to the doctor's for a check-up. I knew that if we didn't go, soon someone would call, and that would be worse. I got dressed. I tidied up Gabrielle's bedroom, and found a shrivelled banana under the mattress.

When Gabrielle came back the cake was gone.

"It was lovely," she said. "Hilary ate most of it. She likes food."

"What does Hilary look like?" I asked conversationally.

"Strange." Gabrielle didn't seem to want to expand.

"Do you climb up the tree to see Hilary?" I asked foolishly.

"Yes. She's made a nest. It's very warm. We curl up."

"Nice," I said weakly.

Then she said:

"Where are you going?"

"To the doctor's."

"But I'm alright!"

I made Gabrielle dress and wash. Her whole body was stiff and unhelpful. In another mood I might have slapped her, but I was tired of fighting.

"I'm worn out," said Gabrielle, and her face was pale. "I think I might be getting a cold."

I wound a scarf round her neck. It was as if she was a baby again. The phone rang loudly. We didn't answer it.

The doctor looked fatalistic. She sat with her broad knees spread before her and quoted medical journals at us for a while. Then she said she wanted to weigh Gabrielle. This is the part we hate. I wanted to say:

"Why don't we weigh you for a change?" I bet her dogs are

fat.

Gabrielle stood on the scales in a trance. She was looking up at the ceiling as if she wanted to fly away. The doctor said:

"It looks to me as if we should have her in."

"I'm not working," I said quickly. "I'm off sick."

"And how is the reward system going?"

I struggled to remember the reward system. It was all about graphs and rules.

"Very well," I lied.

The doctor studied the scales.

"Oh," she said. She sounded disappointed.

"What?"

"The reward system must be working. She's put on two pounds. Well done."

I thought she was going to give me a dog biscuit.

On the way home Gabrielle said:

"What's it like being fat?"

"Nice," I said.

"Hilary's fat."

"Fat and strange eh?"

"Yes, that's right." Gabrielle was pale and serious.

At home my mother had left a note on the door on the back of a Christian postcard. It said:

'Last night we prayed.'

I tore it up, and Gabrielle said:

"I don't want to go to church anymore. They shout too much."

I grinned.

After a fortnight Gabrielle had put on half a stone. It was like watching a baby learn to walk. It even seemed as if our lives went from black and white to colour again. Gradually her face regained some of its features and colours; her arms looked less breakable, her legs plumped out, her eyes were brighter. When mother came round she was victorious. Her prayers were answered, she said. God had moved in mercifully before it was too late. I just nodded dumbly.

I didn't tell my mother about Hilary. Christians don't like imaginary people, apart from the big one. I knew she would disapprove and say that Hilary was the henchwoman of the Anti-Christ.

When she left, eyes raised to the heavens, stamping her way home, I felt bad. I hate it when Christians rejoice. It's worse than when they're miserable. I watched her going down the road in her badly-fitting coat, one arm longer than the other from carrying her bible. I wished that I was a more generous person.

All I cared about was Gabrielle returning to me, fatter and stronger.

I was proud of her.

When Gabrielle was eight-and-a-half stone I applied for a job in a beauty parlour that specialised in anti-ageing products and got the job. It was warm and intimate in the parlour, and I could use the telephone whenever I liked. I had a select and wealthy clientele who treated me with respect, and gave tips in note form.

Gabrielle went back to school. She even began to menstruate. If she spoke of Hilary, I always humoured her. She still took food to the beechwood. I never complained about that either.

As far as I was concerned Gabrielle had cured herself, with the help of her own imagination.

Then one day I came in from work; worn out from sanding down old ladies' wrinkles and plucking bristly old eyebrows, and found Gabrielle in tears in her bedroom. She wouldn't speak. She just kept weeping. It was winter and outside the earth was frosty and white. I thought she must have been bullied at school, or been jilted by some thoughtless lout. I kept on asking her what the matter was until she sat up and said:

"It's Hilary. She's gone all stiff and cold."

I really didn't feel like going out, but I realised that she wouldn't be quiet until I did what she said. We got a torch and walked silently to the wood which was damp and sinister. Gabrielle was holding my hand so tightly that it hurt. I followed her down a brambly path into her private world. I was very nervous. I didn't know what to expect.

We came to a tree that was wide and gnarled. Gabrielle wouldn't let go. She climbed up first and I followed, catching my tights on the branches.

When I saw her I nearly screamed, but the sound stuck in my throat and so I just stared. She was lying in a curl in a nest of rags and bags. She was an old woman dressed in layers and layers of coats and dresses. Her eyes were wide open, and her silver hair coiled around her head in a halo. Her face was peaceful and she was smiling.

Gabrielle whimpered and lay down beside her like an animal seeking warmth. She reached into her pocket and brought out a chocolate bar which he held to Hilary's stiff mouth. I reached out and pulled her hand away. I pulled my own hand gently over Hilary's face, closing the eyes.

It was like turning off a light.

"Who is she?" I said, although I knew.

"She was my friend," sniffed Gabrielle.

There was a small paragraph about Hilary in the local newspaper. No one knew who she was or where she came from. I was afraid that her death would affect Gabrielle, but although she cried a lot she continued to eat.

In time the whole episode seemed dreamlike and insubstantial.

My daughter was saved from death not by a doctor, or by her mother, or by God, but by a woman who lived in a tree.

I feel funny about it sometimes. I dream about Gabrielle curled up snug in the arms of a stranger. I have flashes of jealousy.

And sometimes, when I am patting cream onto the forehead of a client, or waxing a leg, or painting the contours of a cheekbone, I think, it would be nice to stop this, to take off my overall and walk into the quietest, greenest part of a forest, and make a nest, away from everything.

A place just for me.

# The Sack Depot

The window is a flat wet mist and Marcia has been gone for ages. Everything is turned backwards. The wind is blowing in a new direction. Over the dunes I can see the unbleached roots of dune grass. The Sack Depot is confused and tangled. Doors that were once closed are hanging open. I could turn the television on, and make a cup of coffee, but I can't stop hearing how quiet it is. The caravans are hunched together like shipwrecks in the mud.

I saw a long line of people yesterday; their heads bobbing up and down as they stumbled along the bumpy hillocks that hide the sea, all their hair blowing upwards. They were carrying notices, but I can't read words. They had rucksacks and babies with peaked, colourful hats. I ran outside to call them, but the wind was such that it cut my words away as they came out of my mouth. Then I thought I didn't much like the look of them, so I came back and climbed into the cab of a broken-down lorry and sat on the tattered, doggy seat, staring.

Sitting in the trucks was what me and Marcia liked doing best. High up like ladies. Tuning in the radio; smelling the air freshener. Caught in the rumble of the great engine, not having to talk, just watching over the little people by the side of the road.

But this truck is like a dead person; a hulk with no soul. All its bones creak in the damp wind. It has no juice left at all, and I am freezing cold, just sitting here, waiting for Marcia.

I have never been alone before.

When I went to school I tried to make the teacher love me. Mrs. Grassnot. She had lean equal legs with nylons on. I would reach out to touch them, and pinch the elbow of her silky blouse. I could feel her flinch. My right hand has two long fingers and a fat unruly thumb. My left leg is a dangle of unused muscle. Of course there was the usual ribbing. In the playground I kept the others away by twisting my face into grisly expressions and spitting. I was the daily peep show. Sometimes the nursery kids would cry and be scared. Their parents complained that they awoke at night with nightmares.

In the end I took to wagging off with Marcia; climbing the dusty coastal paths in the afternoon and smoking behind dry stone walls. The Wag Wife called round a few times to the Sack Depot, but she was put off by the mud and dogs, and no one read the letters that came with typewritten labels. Anyway, I'm sixteen now, and Marcia is twenty, so we can do what we like.

Marcia has lived with us since she was ten. She is my second cousin. She is big. She has a long wide face like a plate and she wears spectacles. Her hair is like seaweed. Sometimes I comb it. We worked for Uncle Frank, doing the sacks. We sewed the bottoms and blanket-stitched the tops. Sacking was Uncle Frank's sideline. Sometimes he went off to do his real job, and we were left in charge. We wore black and white checky aprons under our anoraks, and fed the dogs. Even the dogs have gone now. I never realised how much they barked, or how much time they took up.

When we had done each sack we tied them into bundles with binder twine and put them on pallets ready for the drivers. Each bundle had a label with the name of a driver written on it. There were green sacks, and white sacks and dirty old brown sacks. They smelt of oil and rope. My hands got quicker and quicker at making them. I could sew a sack up with my eyes closed. Sometimes, when I was working, I would talk to Mrs. Grassnot in my head; show her what I could do, and she would say:

"Well done Sadie. I never knew you could sew sacks like that. We'll show the rest of the class shall we?"

Still, it wasn't a proper job. Even I knew that proper jobs are for a reason. You get wages. We never got wages. We just got cups of coffee and cigarettes off the drivers.

Me and Marcia had names for the drivers. Some we liked and some we didn't. They would sit on boxes in the yard smirking and making jokes that we couldn't understand. There was Mars, who ate Mars Bars, and Pluto, like a duck, and Venus who was a flirt, and Harpie who played the mouth organ, and Steve.

Mars had a long tongue, like a snake, and thin hair. Pluto was nearly as ugly as Uncle Frank and skinny as a starved dog. Venus was always beckoning and whispering words we didn't understand. Harpie was fat and red, like uncooked sausage, and Steve was nice. He was like a man on television. He wore a jacket with a sheepskin collar. I felt hot whenever he was in the yard. Everything he said sounded nice.

"Two sugars" or "Thanks a million."

The other drivers called him Kiddo, but I never nicknamed him. I just called him Steve.

It's nearly night now. I am still here. All I can hear is seagulls and that makes me feel homesick, though I am at home, but now home is different. It's as cold as the school railings, as Mrs. Grassnot's eyes, as sitting watching the other children play games, or on the apparatus with their smooth whole limbs and quick little fingers.

One time. It was hot. Midsummer. All the flies danced around the sacks and the dogs hung their tongues out. I could smell myself through my overall. Marcia was flopping about like an old fat seal. She had tied a scarf round her big middle to make her skirt shorter, and her legs wobbled and stuck together.

The drivers were larking about with a hose; putting it between their legs and spraying each other. Me and Marcia wanted to join in but didn't know how. We just stood there chewing gum and snuckling with each other. Then Venus nudged one of the others and they all looked at us, and I knew the spotlight was on me and something was going to happen.

Venus said, "Fancy a walk Sadie?" and Steve looked uncomfortable and said, "Leave off man!"

"I've got something to show you," Venus said, and all the other drivers looked uncomfortable and the hose just lay on the ground with water spilling out of it into a puddle.

"What?" I said, remembering the faces I used to make in the playground, and wondering if that would make Venus laugh and change the subject.

"I'll go with you," said Marcia, stepping away from me.

"Will you now?" Venus had crocodile eyes. One of the dogs snapped at a fly.

Marcia tripped away in the direction of the string twister; a corrugated iron hut which hung precariously onto one side of an empty caravan. Venus followed; looking back at the others, shrugging his shoulders, while they seemed to have forgotten Marcia, him and me, and were looking at the ground, rubbing their boots into the ashy gravel.

Next thing I heard was Marcia's shrill laugh. Her and Venus were inside the hut. Behind the laugh was fear. Only I knew this. Marcia's laugh was meant to be not bothered, but I knew different. You don't spend hours with someone behind dry stone walls without knowing something of their inner lives. Marcia was scared.

I went to the string twister and poked my head around the uneven doorway.

"Marcia?" I said.

Venus was lurking in the corner, his Elvis hairstyle silhouetted against a dirty window frame.

"What IS it Sadie?" said Marcia, trying to be unfriendly.

"Come here a minute. I've got something to tell you."

39

Marcia sighed, as if I was a difficult, whining child, and whispered something to Venus that sounded sweaty and difficult.

Then she sidled outside, messing about with her buttons and pulling down her skirt, looking sullen.

That's when I locked Venus in the string twister. Marcia looked shocked, and then she started to giggle. I wrapped binder twine round and round the door handle. Venus was struggling with the catch. He must have accidentally touched the button that operated the machine, and the hut began to whir, and the chimney started to smoke. Marcia was really laughing now. Tears were running down her cheeks in squeezed drops. She ran up the bank, clutching her huge belly.

Then all the drivers came running to the hut. They looked like wild horses; all their eyes large and white. Harpie broke the door down with his broad shoulder, and I suddenly knew not to look, so I ran after Marcia.

There were plenty of questions to answer after that. Questions with words like aforesaid and unfortunate. The police took Marcia into a separate room, and when she came out she looked pink and unhappy. But it was Venus who switched on the button, not me. All I did was wind the twine around the doorhandle. I kept on saying the same words over and over again until they sent us home. For a while I had a social worker called Irene who patted my good hand a lot and got me a new stick. I might have liked her more if she had stayed a bit longer. In the end she started to look like Mrs. Grassnot, and that made me feel angry. Once when she came I wouldn't come down from sitting in the driver's seat of a lorry, and I could see she was annoyed. The top of her head was grassy and dry. I wanted to drop something on it. She said she would come back, but she hasn't yet.

Marcia sang "Irene, goodnight Irene!" and I should have laughed, but I didn't.

It's dark now. Outside I can hear animals running beneath the truck. I light a tab end and it fizzes red light over my hand. My fingers are dirty with grease around the fingernails. I keep worrying about Marcia, running across the wide white beach, with her overall flapping. I hope she has kept her head and not forgotten the things we said. I realise I have never seen Marcia use a telephone, or light an oil lamp, or have a sensible conversation. She has been gone for a whole night and a day. I can't run like Marcia, or I would have gone. She has limbs and I have sense.

Up until the accident I had been someone who smiled often. Mrs. Grassnot would snap, "wipe that grin off your face, Sadie, it isn't funny." I don't know where I learnt to smile; not at the depot or in the playground. Maybe the wind blew and my face got stuck. The accident changed my face though. I stopped smiling, and became depressed. I couldn't sew the sacks properly anymore, and without thinking I stitched them together, or embroidered stars on them instead. Uncle Frank got sick of me, and shouted loudly at me so that everyone heard. The dogs howled at the same time. Mars wouldn't speak to me at all, and Pluto and Harpie were edgy and acted as if I was bad luck. Steve once squeezed my shoulder and asked me where my smile had gone. I told him the truth; that it was twisted up in the string twister.

In the middle of this misery the men from the ministry walked down the track.

The first one was an eagle, with high shoulders and a long brown back. He muttered his way around the depot while Uncle Frank loitered behind a rusty tractor in the backyard. We all stood there watching the man, our lips curling every time he moved. The dogs growled. I showed him the place where the string twister had been, but he wasn't interested in that. He was interested in buying the Sack Depot for the new government building. I thought

41

he meant offices, but he didn't. He meant another kind of depot, which would be modern and efficient and powerful. It was going to be huge, he said, and would fill up all the land that we could see. He paced up and down, counting, writing down figures in a clip file.

Then another one came. This one had a great pink baby face and a baldy head. His cheeks ballooned outwards, as if he had been inflated with air. He floated down the muddy driveway and caught Uncle Frank coming out of the Sack Hut. He spoke angrily and kept saying the same thing.

"September twelfth!" He didn't say September THE twelfth, which Mrs. Grassnot would have said in her clear haughty voice, just, "September twelfth."

Uncle Frank threw things around after he had gone. It was August then, and heavy bees hung in the hedges. The beach was full of squirming couples and sad men on their own. We ate our meals in silence in the caravan.

I began to smoke full time.

The calendar that hung in the depot office with a naked, thumb- marked girl looking down from it had a rough pencil ring drawn around this looming date. When September twelfth arrived Uncle Frank told me and Marcia to get lost.

He had never been so direct.

"Get lost!" he said, and gave us a fiver.

We took a flask and went down to the dunes. We walked further than we had ever done before. We took off our shoes and went looking for starfish in rockpools. We sang hymns we remembered from school, lying on our backs on the hard sand. Then we rolled over and drew pictures with sticks of beautiful women in flowing clothes and lay on them; pressing ourselves down into their bodies.

Then, when the sand was quite cold and the sea no longer blue, we began to traipse back over the spikey grass, holding hands like lovers; ambling and limping and stopping for shivering rests.

It was night when we got here. The depot was deserted. It looked as if there had been a war. Sacks lay everywhere looking confused, as if they had risen up to fight the ministry men and been defeated. The caravans were splintered and broken, and pots and pans and broken mugs and plates lay on the grass.

We didn't know what to do then. I felt as if there was no one else alive in the world; just me and Marcia, who sat crying on a box. That's when I told her to go and get help, while I waited for Uncle Frank to come back. I remembered that all the drivers' telephone numbers were written on a piece of cardboard in the office. I told Marcia to phone Steve, and tell him to come and get us.

And Marcia went, wiping her spectacles and nodding her unwise head.

I can hear singing coming from the beach. There's the glow of a fire and sparks rising above the dunes. I clamber down from the truck, pick up an oil lamp, light it, and start walking towards the sound. I am so cold I can't even feel the wind anymore; all I can hear is this chanting. When I get to the dune edge I look down at a circle of people sitting there. It's the same people who were trudging along before. They sing "We Shall Not Be Moved" and all of them are grinning. Then I see Mrs. Grassnot. She's wearing a woolly hat and a big jumper. She stands up and sings louder than anyone else, "THIS LAND IS OUR LAND!"

Everyone is standing up and joining in. They have apple cheeks and strong arms and legs.

Then I get mad. I stand up on the dune and shout down at them:

"WIPE THOSE GRINS OFF! IT'S MY LAND, D'YOU HEAR! THIS IS WHERE I LIVE!"

Then they stop singing and look up at me, and I know that they can't see me. I am just a dark shape yelling nonsense in the grass; a stray dog, howling.

They're frightened though.

Then a light suddenly arcs over the sky, and there is a noise like an earthquake behind me. I don't move. It's like being on a stage, all lit up, like a star. They gaze at me, their faces blank and surprised.

"Sadie!" A voice calls across the fret.

"Sadie, it's me ! I found a telephone!"

I turn then. Marcia is calling from the cab of a great beautiful truck. Steve is sitting beside her in the drivers seat and the radio is playing Tamla Motown.

"Come on!" she yells.

I stumble and drag myself over to the cab and climb the mountain of steps. I feel as if I'm climbing up to heaven.

Then I look down, one last time, straight into the eyes of Mrs. Grassnot, plump and hot in her sheepwool, and stick two fingers up, and the string in my face starts to unravel.

And I sing, "THIS LAND IS MY LAND, THIS LAND IS MY LAND," for a long time, until Marcia tells me to shut up.

# Affliction

Love is electric. It fills a house with static. It lights up the night, and forbids sleep. I had that experience; but it lost its vital elements, and gradually dimmed until I was forced to find another source of power.

I was afflicted by a person called Jet, who had been reared by New Age travellers, and had dark shining hair like an otter, and white hands. It was quite extraordinary and shocking. We met at an Italian class, in the rotting back rooms of a university. We had to converse about the weather in pairs. That's when it happened. It was like being drunk for months. Jet and I disrupted the class with our charged relationship. I know now how boring it must have been for Mrs Benini, who struggled through eight weeks of our covert caresses and inappropriate laughter. We stank of sex and no one would sit near us. Magical things happened to me. I even began to speak fluent Italian. When the class ended we rented a flat together and on the first night we lay on the floor and listened to opera music while the neighbours banged on the ceiling and the floor, cursing us.

Jet played the piano. It was a small flat and the instrument took up most of the sitting room. I didn't mind that. I liked to imagine the keyboard was my spine. The sound of the piano filled the whole flat. It was a blunt, complete sound. I never touched it. I got pregnant.

The pregnancy had an immediate effect on our great romance. Jet used a kind of scented hair oil that gave off a profound and dominating smell. It made me want to vomit. I said:

"Can you stop using that hair oil," but Jet didn't answer and that was our first real disagreement. It was a small thing but as I grew lumpy and drab the smell pervaded everything and I often had to go out and roam round supermarkets just to get away from it.

Then I started to think Jet was laughing at me. I was not one of those women who blossom in gestation. I lost interest in my appearance. Domestically I was inept, and so was Jet. The flat became infested with cockroaches that I could hear chuckling at night. I could even hear them in the piano, making the strings warble in ghostly chords. Jet often stayed out late and by the time the door scraped open I was so cracked that my voice would ooze out in long miserable whines. We were no longer in Italy and the light bulbs kept going.

When Daphne was born Jet bought me a bunch of daffodils and sang to me in the hospital. I knew I was supposed to smile and be radiant, but I just thought about my nipples and if they would ever heal, and when Jet went I limped to the lounge and smoked three cigarettes with a woman called Bella who had just had her sixth boy. Bella, who was a tent of a woman with a face like an eider-down gave me a book to read. It was called *A Kiss In The Dark*. I read it that night while all the other birthing women groaned uncomfortably in their state beds. It was a classic love book, in which characters melted into one another and brushed their lips all over the place, like brooms. The author had started writing when she was forty.

When I got home Jet had polished the piano and made the beds. I sat on the floor with Daphne and looked through a catalogue while Jet made a saucepan of weak soup. I ordered an electric typewriter, and asked Jet to post the letter.

"What do you want a typewriter for?" jeered Jet, whose good intentions were beginning to slip.

"I thought I might write a book," I said soupily.

"You!"

That was the first time I realised that Jet despised me.

The typewriter arrived - I am still paying five pounds a week for it - and when Daphne slept I struggled with romantic prose. I would hide the work from Jet, but sometimes it would get discovered and Jet would read out chunks in a falsetto voice and mock my fragile intentions. It was as if the very act of writing was somehow an insult to our relationship.

"What makes you think anyone will want to read this?" sneered Jet, after lampooning my first literary sexual encounter.

I thought of the Italian Class then. I had passed and could have continued to an advanced level, whereas Jet had failed miserably. At the time we had torn up the results and fallen into a soggy embrace under a nearby university willow tree.

Jet's tongue, which once had travelled the length and breadth of my body, now found its passion in vindictive words. Jet had a job now, and we had an ansafone and a set of Le Creuset saucepans.

I couldn't afford to be affected by this kind of petty nastiness; I had too much to think about; romantic terminology, Daphne, and killing cockroaches.

A year passed, and once again a bunch of daffodils stood calmly in a vase on the piano; but this time I had bought them for myself to celebrate the finishing of "She Came In The Lift." The manuscript was in a new brown envelope in the shopping tray of Daphne's pram. We strolled down to the post office and defiantly posted it to a publishing house, with an address as long as the queue of prams waiting to cash their child benefit. When Jet came home the desk was abnormally neat.

"Where is the great work?" snapped Jet.

"Gone." I had grown skilled at one word answers.

"Gone where?"

"Courtney Watts... it's a publishers."

"Do you really think that anyone would seriously..." But I had stopped listening. I was thinking about a sequel. I mean, I didn't think I was clever or anything, but I did like romance. I needed it. It stopped me from pulverising Daphne who had started to be as obsessive as a primadonna. It would have been no use saying that to Jet, who would have merely scorned my maternal failings.

These days Jet bought suits from Burtons and worked as a peripatetic music teacher. He seemed to want to forget his roots and never spoke of his mother who still trailed the motorways of Britain searching for a field of clover.

That month I met a woman called Audrey in a butcher's shop. I was trying to buy a pound of sausages and she was an animal liberationist who was leafleting the customers. She had a baby with her, slung round her neck, with its greedy mouth turned into the moist folds of her teeshirt.

I returned the sausages after she made me feel queasy with her lurid propaganda, and we started talking in the way that mothers do; a dreamy kind of chat that is half supportive, half competitive. After that I kept meeting her in the street and at the doctors and once she burst into tears, because she said, she didn't get enough sleep, and it was so important to campaign now for the rights of animals. That's how we started looking after each other's children; so we could pursue our particular passions. Jet really hated that. He said Daphne was being corrupted by a maniac. What irked Jet most though, was my ability to concentrate; for now I was really in the languid land of hot words and my next book was a sexual orgy from start to seedy finish.

Then, one chilly breakfast, a letter arrived from Courtney Watts, the publisher, who had been so silent that I believed that perhaps my first book had ceased to exist.

Jet sat opposite me eating a boiled egg while I neatly sliced open the white envelope with the bread knife. He was watching me closely with his lashed rodent eyes. He held a teaspoon of yellow yolk a distance from his mouth as I read aloud:

*Dear Ms Grey* (that is my sad name*)*
*We read your manuscript "She Came In The Lift" with great delight, and we would very much like to include it in our Autumn Catalogue. Could you contact us at the first possible opportunity...*

I read no further. I jumped up and howled with passionate joy. Jet's eyes widened and Daphne screamed and knocked over a pint of milk. I started dabbing up the milk with Jet's newspaper, smiling and jabbering. Jet was laughing so hard he dropped egg yolk on his tie, and he ran to the tap and scrubbed it with a nail brush. It was quiet then, just the tap running, and Daphne watching, and the letter lying in the toast crumbs. Then Jet said:

"Pleased are you?"

"Of course I am!" I whispered. Something was wrong. Jet's mouth was curling up at one side, and he was slithering around the kitchen like a wizard in a pantomime.

"What day is it?" Jet stood near the Musician's Union calendar, smacking his lips.

"I don't know," I whimpered.

"Think!" He pointed at the days. I looked. A pinch and a punch for the first of the month.

"You little fool..." Jet whispered.

I turned the letter over slowly. Jet's handwriting in green ink pen had scratched the words "APRIL FOOL" on the white stationery.

I looked at Jet who was grinning and dangling his wet tie above the radiator.

Daphne was sick. Her vomit was yellow and watery.

Jet was apologising.

I realised I was shouting in Italian and started to snigger. Then I picked up Daphne, still dripping with sick, and took a bottle of brandy from the cupboard. I couldn't hear anything that Jet was saying. It was as if his volume had been turned off.

I went to Audrey's. She answered the door with a face like a nun. She had seen it coming a long way off, she said, like a smell.

I stayed there for two days and helped Audrey do a mailing about battery chickens.

I really like Audrey, even though she is a maniac.

When I called home it was only to collect nappies for Daphne and to get some things. Audrey said I could stay in her spare room, and even offered to remove the posters of mad cows.

As soon as I opened the door I knew Jet had gone. The place smelt different. The hair oil had receded and the piano had left a large musty space. The love nest had finally disintegrated, leaving only contented cockroaches and stray human hairs and the dust from our bodies. I packed the typewriter and two carrier bags, then blew one kiss into the lifeless rooms.

On the way out I noticed a letter on the mat addressed to me. I picked it up. It was white and expensive, and the name Courtney Watts was printed on the top.

I put it carefully in my breast pocket, next to my heart, to open with Audrey over wholemeal spaghetti.

# *Wings*

First mother trod on a nail and her foot went septic. Then she found a Bunsen burner alight in her bed, the mattress horribly smelly and melted. After that, it soon became apparent that Bliss was an arsonist and that everything would have to change.

It was a year of accidents. Glorious and sudden. She came to fear the smell of smoulder. There was too much suspense.

By mid-year the whole house stank of sulphur. Casually ripped Swan Vestas boxes littered the hallways. The edges of the carpets were charred; armchairs scalded and frayed. The bedding had a smoky odour and the windows appeared sooty from within.

Mother wore a fire extinguisher clipped to her apron and converted the heating to electricity.

After the televised version of Jane Eyre, Bliss became extraordinary - fond of ceremony rather than mere flame. She began to dance around small pyres of twigs doused in paraffin, her flame-resistant nightie flapping in the sparks.

How she learned these skills was a mystery. Mother believed in demons and alien infiltration. She was ashamed.

She was afraid of Social Services and the women at the tennis club. She prayed to the stars instead.

Babysitters were out of the question.

Life was hot.

Bliss blossomed, lingering around the electric cooker with pockets full of crumbling firelighters while mother eyed her with gloom.

Each day Mother and Bliss walked by the cool river. It was a short walk; a walk that was intentionally dull, along a tarmac path that opened into a wider, dreary track; the river doomed, shrouded with exhausted trees, the ducks unintelligent.

The path despaired eventually and became a car park. Here they turned and walked back through a nursery garden, pausing to watch rows of lettuce, or broad beans in various stages of neat growth. Mother hoped to tame her child with these quiet forays into quotidian life.

But the year was not yet up. One afternoon, suddenly, a swan reared up from the river and charged at Bliss with watery venom. It wasn't as bad as it could have been. A mere peck on the arm and a white wing shutting out the sun. A few seconds. But Bliss turned quite white. White as a wing.

Mother was not good at sympathy. At home the quietness hung like river mist. Bliss thought only of the necks of swans and forgot fires. Mother sank into a smile and washed the windows.

On Christmas Day, Mother was nearly happy. A thin sheet of picturesque snow covered the hard earth. She had arrayed the house with daring paper decorations, and even lit a candle in the front window, so that passers-by could feel the warmth of Christmas time.

In the morning Mother gave Bliss a doll with blue eyes that looked bleakly into the middle distance. Bliss gave her mother a picture in a plastic frame. She had drawn it herself. It was a grey picture of a river lined with poplar trees. Mother shed tears of gratitude.

Then, setting their presents aside, Mother suggested a walk before lunch, not noticing how Bliss's eyes also looked out into the middle distance. Bliss nodded. Secretly Mother wanted to say a secret thankyou to the swan.

Once again treading the tedious river track, she pointed out how calm the swans looked riding the dirty river upstream, but Bliss merely felt the inside of her pockets, and the red sulphur tips of loose matches. Mother said the swans belonged to the Queen, although no doubt they did much as they liked.

And Bliss watched the imperceptible falling of white snow and remembered the shock of the swan bite - the sensation that had put out her fire, her passion. She raged against the boredom of her eight years; the formica of the kitchen, the pattern of the carpet in the living room, the neat dressing table in her bedroom.

She felt sorry for the woman in the grey woollen coat who walked beside her. She was convinced that she wasn't her mother. A real mother would put her arms about her and love her. A real mother would never have called her Bliss. Something was terribly wrong.

It was uncharacteristic of Mother to lunge into the nursery garden and pick up a poinsettia. Bliss, left unguarded for a short wing of a second, flickered away, running to a shed that stood teetering on the edge of the river bank.

The swans gathered by the sluice, rummaging in the water with their necks curving dangerously, like snakes constrained in feathers. They looked up at Bliss with mean eyes.

Mother carried the poinsettia to the till and absently felt an empty breeze around her skirts. Then she smelt the old secure scent of paraffin and saw a twist of black smoke curling like a smile into the sky.

The shed burnt so quickly. Like a matchbox set alight, it tore into flame, falling down in sparkly gulps into the river, onto swans, onto beaks and white feathers. They flapped.

And Bliss roared with sad laughter at the swans' confusion. Matches in her hand. Hands in her pockets.

Mother just stood there, hands twisted around her red and green plant, sighing; as if a planetary omen had come true, as if Social Services and the people from the car park knew everything there was to know.

For a moment the warmth of flames fanned her, and as she dropped her poinsettia, she saw her past years as a great grey wave behind her, and knew that changes must be made in the wake of this and all other catastrophes.

Later when she told this story, many years later, she laughed and laughed until the tears ran down her cheeks.

And the only other thing to remark upon was the smell of Christmas dinner.

# Floor Wax

Her earliest years were the best.

Anna was reared on the smell of floor wax and polish, in a flat in the centre of a proud and dirty city with gold plates on its doors; and a river full of ships that carried diamonds, coal and guns; and stone cherubs and embossed marble ceilings; and cafes that served bacon grease soup and gritty chips.

Anna was blind.

Her days were cacophonies of wailing sirens, of shouting men who dredged the coaly mud, of cranes that creaked, of rough wartime underwear and green soap made from whale blubber; of fragile hairnets and resonant brass bands, and dark nights and slow asthmatic trains and hard leather seats.

Anna's mother Ursula was not poor. She lived in a block of apartments not far from the noisy river, with a vast tiled lobby and an ebony lift that cranked up the insides of the building at such a slow speed that there was time to darn a stocking between the ground and the top floor.

Each morning the lobby was cleaned by anonymous women with buckets and grey cloths, and polished with beeswax and spit.

Ursula was half-Polish and a confectioner. Warsaw was still in her consonants, although her vowels were more English than the Queen.

Anna's father had gone away on business; disappearing into the criss-cross map of middle Europe, like a lost brown telegram. Once a month a cheque would arrive for Ursula, with a letter that smelt of velvet and cognac. The letters were about the weather. At the bottom there were kisses for his daughter that Ursula would count on Anna's fingers.

At Anna's seventh birthday party there were three aunts, Ursula and a cousin called June with the voice of a pea. There was a shop gateau, with a ballerina dancing stiffly on the top, that tasted of cardboard. Anna wore a dress that rustled like a moth in a wardrobe.

The aunts talked of her father with gusts of emptiness in their voices. Even his name, Frederick, was an old brown sail flapping. Anna never knew the shape of his face; only that when he returned for short formal visits the atmosphere changed, and the flat smelt of barber shops, and that his voice was muffled and awkward and that he never knew what to say.

Ursula was not herself when he was there. She became rather childish. After Frederick had gone she was all sugar and pins. She brought paper bags home filled with crushed sweet cakes. Her voice was creamy and soft again.

She would lean over Anna and kiss her, and afterwards Anna would lick the sugar off her mouth left there by Ursula's lips. It was like growing up in a gingerbread house.


On Sundays Aunts Olga, Hannah and Birgitte would come to tea, and it would seem as if a starched cloth fell from the sky onto the dining-room table. Their spoons rattled in their china teacups when they stirred their tea. Sometimes Anna smelt envy on their clothes, which were cheap and threadbare. The aunts lived in the grey district beyond the railway station. They had thin painted lips and chipped teeth. Anna could hear their bones aching beneath their clothes. They ate very slowly, and Ursula offered them too much too quickly. Their sons had all left home. They spoke of them like long distance lorries; big and gone. Only June was left.

After tea the family would walk in the park. Ursula was the leader in her fox wrap, and the aunts walked behind her in cast-off coats. Anna held her mother's hand through warm kid gloves. She could feel her wedding ring through the smooth leather.

When they could hear the brass band, Anna knew they were near the swings, which squealed with pain the higher you went.

All the time Ursula would talk; telling her what there was to be seen, and filling in the inner image that Anna carried of her small world.

"A couple is passing. They seem sad, or perhaps they have just over-eaten. A child has fallen off the swing. Can you hear how loudly she cries Anna? She has made her dress all dirty up the back. A dog is barking at a squirrel, but the squirrel doesn't care."

Anna pictured Ursula as an empress, her features noble as a king, her stature evident to all who passed. She almost believed that ordinary people must bow to her as she walked through the city park; that men everywhere would desire her, but that she would shake her head, preferring a quiet existence with Anna and the weekly contact with her husband's sisters. Anna was as secure as the strong iron bridge that crossed the city river.

That is, until she was eight, when Frederick sent a larger cheque and Ursula found a doctor.

The sweet atmosphere began to change and there was a new sour taste in the air. For many months Anna went to the clinic out of town, where Doctor Reddish tinkled his metal instruments and stood so close to her that she could smell the tobacco on his clothes. His hands were hairy and dry, and they turned her head this way and that until her neck ached. She felt the heat of torch-light on her face, and answered his questions in a frightened voice.

Ursula would stand by the door, her voice patchy and uncertain. Aunts Olga, Birgitte and Hannah came to tea less often. June was at school.

There were fewer treats and less cake, and it seemed to Anna that everyone was working harder and laughing less.

Then one day Anna was taken with her night-clothes in a leather suitcase, to a hospital, and put to bed, although she felt perfectly healthy. The bed-linen was icy against her skin, and the nurses glided about silently, making her jump when they spoke. Anna cried loudly for her mother, and threw a glass of water against a wall, so that it smashed into splinters and frightened other patients, that Anna hadn't known were there. She lay down then, defeated and confused, and offered her thin arm for an injection.

When Anna awoke she vomited into a metal bowl. Her head felt as if it was charged with minute batteries, and tight bandages were wrapped around her eyes. They made her lie still for days. She hummed brass band tunes flatly and made imaginary cakes. Slowly, light, colour and shape began to filter through the bandages in ominous shadows.

Finally, a day came when Ursula and the three aunts came to her bedside, their voices strained and cheery.

"We have a surprise for you," Ursula said wildly.

Doctor Reddish unwound the stiff cotton bandage.

The first thing that Anna saw was her mother's chin. It had a large purple mole on it. She looked up and saw that Ursula was not beautiful; her eyes were small and her nose was long. Next to her stood a man in a heavy gabardine coat with a beard and nervous eyes.

"This is your father," her mother said. "Look at him. He paid for this."

She couldn't; she turned to her aunts instead, who were scrawny and distempered with yellow teeth. Anna wept.

The four women laughed. It was joy, they said, that made her cry. But Anna wept with disillusionment. Her father was a stranger. Everything; the ward, the other patients, the sky outside the window, even her own face, was a disappointment. Ursula

58

tried to take a photograph of the moment with an old Brownie camera, but Anna would not smile and hid under the covers. Doctor Reddish said that she was suffering from shock, and told her to sleep. When she woke and her relations were gone, she was afraid to open her eyes.

When she returned home from hospital there was a newer photograph of Frederick on the mantelpiece, and a bunch of wilting roses with a card from him to Anna on the table. One of her first sighted memories was petals dropping one by one onto the shining wood.

The flat, that had seemed luxurious in her imagination, was small, shabby and untidy. Ursula's fox fur was moth-eaten.

Anna's state of confusion abated but never quite disappeared. She grew up frowning; never quite lifting her eyes up to the light. She helped her mother ice the stodgy cakes for the front window of the small shop. She went to school wearing a pair of heavy spectacles and sat in the front row watching the chalk squeak across the blackboard. She learnt to swim. She read Jane Austen and Charles Dickens, and sometimes she shut her eyes and re-membered the exotic smells of her childhood: polish and coffee, demerara sugar and fox wrap, glace cherries, and the darker back-ground smell of coal and river.

One day, when Anna was fifteen, a letter arrived with stamps littered across it haphazardly in rows. Her mother sat in an arm-chair and read it over and over again. Eventually she said to Anna:

"Your father is dead," and placed the letter on the mantelpiece. Anna shrugged. The cheques stopped arriving.

After that her mother became pale and melancholic. Sugar was rationed, and she turned to baking cheap savouries. Her hair turned grey and she sometimes complained of bad feet, bad back and bad head. She was short-tempered with Anna and looked at her accusingly, as if she expected something.

When her mother married Gilbert, Anna was relieved. He was stout, with whisky cheeks and sorrowful hands. He worked for a bank, and his fingers were copper green from handling money. He was generous, kind and gallant, and sang in a male voice choir. He was also boring.

The aunts were mesmerised by him, always looking at him curiously, as if trying to understand his masculinity. They sniggered when he spoke to them. He treated them with magnanimity, offering them small liqueurs and putting cushions behind their backs. Within six months he was as permanent as the dining room table; and mutual respect hung over the apartment in thin cigar smoke. Yet Anna saw them as a quiet, melancholic couple, full of sadnesses and regrets. She tiptoed around them and felt big and clumsy in their presence. At sixteen she was gaunt and dull. She listened to the radio and did her homework.

Then on her seventeenth birthday Gilbert gave her a camera. Her mother gave her a watch, and her aunts clubbed together and bought her a silver bracelet. Her cousin June, who had grown up to be fat and vivacious, gave her a box of fudge.

On the night of Anna's birthday Ursula burst into tears after Anna had gone to bed, telling Gilbert that her daughter had no friends and wouldn't look her in the eye. Gilbert agreed. It was like living with a grey cloud. She was worse than some of the people who worked at the bank.

After Anna had eaten the fudge and put the watch and the bracelet in a box beneath her bed, she looked uneasily through the viewer of the camera. It had a curious effect on her. It made her feel something, although she couldn't describe what. She felt oddly in control. For some days she walked around the city with the camera in her satchel, taking it out and looking, then replacing it furtively. The messy colours and shapes before her took on a new meaning when seen through a rectangle.

She began to plan photographs, minutely and carefully. Photographs of streets and bridges, rivers and skylines, cranes and buildings.

Soon she had become obsessed. She took film after film; filling photograph albums, and spending any pocket money she had on her new hobby.

She made the cupboard under the stairs into a dark room, and was rarely seen in daylight. The whole apartment stank of chemicals.

When she eventually emerged, to ask if her mother would pay for her to go to college, Ursula shook her head, saying that Anna must help her in the shop. Then Gilbert stepped in, offering to pay himself. It was nearly an argument, but Gilbert squeezed Ursula's hand and she stopped herself from protesting and instead made Anna thank him profusely. Secretly she wished that Anna would thank her instead. Hadn't she brought her up all alone? She wondered why her daughter always made her feel guilty.

Anna went to college and studied photography. When she graduated, her tutors praised her work enthusiastically, but even their voices were weightless against Anna's silence.

A week before her degree show, Gilbert collapsed at his sixtieth birthday party; too drunk on whisky and soda to feel any pain, the table laden with rich pastries and the guests from the bank mid-toast. The aunts clung to one another like orphans, and Ursula sank into an armchair moaning. Anna covered him up with a tartan rug and phoned an ambulance, but he was already dead.

Ursula never saw Anna's final show. She seemed to be covered with an invisible dust sheet, and the aunts flapped around her, red eyed and insubstantial.

Anna left home.

As she walked out through the tiled lobby she met Aunt Birgitte carrying a Swiss roll in a string bag. The inevitable shadow of

Aunts Hannah and Olga slid up behind her.

"Going far?" asked Birgitte bitterly.

Anna couldn't think of anything to say. She walked past them, leaving a trail of accusatory whispers.

Her photographs were sometimes in magazines. Ursula would buy them and touch the glossy surface sadly with her fingertips. Anna rarely phoned. Sometimes she would come to tea on Sunday, and the conversation would be fragmented and awkward.

The aunts would talk about her afterwards whilst washing up the tea cups.

"Why won't she take photographs of her family?" they said to each other. "Why is she so cold?  What have we ever done to her?"

Ursula sat in the armchair, staring bleakly at photographs on the mantelpiece.

One Sunday Ursula suddenly put her head in her hands and started to sob. The aunts looked horrified. Anna said stiffly:

"What's the matter with you?"

"I can't see," Ursula wailed. "I can't see anything."

After that Anna came every week. She arrived earlier than the aunts and would sit opposite Ursula for an hour before tea. Often she couldn't think of anything to say. Often Ursula forgot that she was there.

One day Ursula said, "Are you there Anna?"

"Yes," she replied.

"Sometimes, when I'm sitting here, I can smell your father, like a scent I once wore; but then you are quite like him."

"What do you mean?"

"Cold."

Ursula pulled a shawl around her.

"I don't mean to be," Anna whispered. She hated it when Ursula tried to talk about emotional things. She wanted to change the subject.

"We only slept together twice," Ursula said. "We had to get married; because of you, because of people. He lived with another woman, in Berlin. A woman with golden hair, very young, very feminine. A woman who never worked for a living. I made him pay. I made him pay all his life."

Anna felt like crying.

"Anna, what can you see?." Ursula leant towards her.

"I don't know what you mean."

"What can you see?"

"The table, you, the pattern of the wallpaper, the view out of the window."

"What else? Go on." She was like a child asking for a story.

"The light is very dim," said Anna. "Your hair is nearly white."

"Oh dear," said Ursula. She paused and turned her head towards the doorway.

"I can smell floorwax; can you smell it?"

"Floorwax?"

"Polish, and scent. Are you wearing scent?"

"A little."

"And I can smell the next door neighbour having a bath."

Later on, on her way out, Anna stopped in the tiled lobby, but all she could smell was the modern odours of Flash and Vim. It occurred to Anna that maybe smells lingered over decades, and that Ursula was smelling the past.

That night she drank a bottle of wine and saw things through Ursula's blind eyes.

Anna made a decision. For the first time she loaded colour film into her camera. The next morning she went to her aunts' house. They were sitting watching television in a tiny sitting room. When she told them she wanted to photograph them, they skipped upstairs and dressed up in Marks and Spencers suits and brushed their hair. It was, Anna thought, as if they had been waiting for her to see them for over twenty years. They stood smiling in a row outside the garden gate, giggling like schoolgirls. They were so old that they had to lean against one another to stand up.

Then Anna went to the small cake shop, which was now run by June and seemed completely eclipsed by modern buildings all around it. June held a pink cake proudly for the portrait.

At last Anna returned to Ursula, who seemed to have nearly disappeared into the voluminous armchair.

She leant over her and kissed her on the forehead.

"How do I look?" asked Ursula.

"Beautiful," said Anna.

# The Street

I can tell a good sausage from a poor one by putting it to my ear.

I was in the sausage shop when a stranger glided in. He said he was after a woman called Amy Steel, and that's me.

I didn't like the look of him. He smelt of brown paper envelopes, and civic corridors. I shook my head at the butcher and he told the visitor that he didn't know me. Also, I don't like meeting strangers in my slippers, and if I was in trouble, I wanted time to get ready. I turned and ran back home and put on support tights and pearl lipstick and sat waiting, pursing my furry old lips and looking out of the window that overlooks my street. It was unusually quiet. The dogs weren't barking, the babies weren't yelling.

I held my front door keys firmly in my hand, which is my way of being alert, and wondered what was about to happen. I'm known as a trouble-maker. Every day I complain about something. There's no shortage of matters to complain about. No one ever listens, and the more silent the officials are the more I complain. Perhaps this has finally dawned on the men in suits, hence the visitor.

Whenever I sit down, which isn't often, I consider the past. It's like a jigsaw that I'm always trying to get straight. I could see one of my nieces lifting her nets and staring at me. I had a feeling she was whispering about me to someone else. I closed my eyes and thought.

The street is long. Once it was a dirt track with a few rotting houses propped up either side. Now it's brick and mortar, and I oversee the cleaning of the pavements and the polishing of the windows. I was born here. A wild bull ran up my mother's stairs and got into bed with her. I am the result of that union. That's what makes me different. If it wasn't for me there wouldn't be a street, every single person in this row has some of my blood in them.

I complain about the state of the pavements, the wildness of the dogs, and the scruffy street sign that hangs off the house at the end. Sometimes I feel that my life has been a battle against abandonment, against the clouds of dust that keep settling over and over again, and against men and destruction. It seems to me that there are two kinds of woman; mad or bad. I am the second kind.

I was born before multi-storeys existed, when schools were inkwells, and women wrapped sticks into bundles and exchanged them for meat bones.

I'm so old now that my face is an ordnance survey map. You could find your way home by it. It's full of streets and hills and valleys and chimneys. I was the oldest child of thirteen children, which makes me special. I've been looking after babies since I was a baby myself.

They told me I was clever at school, but I knew that I must fail at arithmetic and English and geography, because there was no room for those things in my life. If I had passed and tried to continue with my education then it would have been no use. Ma would have rolled my schoolbooks into fire-lighters, and the words would have become smoke smogging up the sky.

I left school at fourteen and went away, to work at a hospital in the countryside. It was a place for poor women who were trying to forget. We did a lot of sluicing, and because we were young, we larked about, as there was nothing else to do in the country. All you could see through the windows was fields. I came home sometimes on the bus, which was filled with young girls who were maids and farmhands, and who carried parcels of food home to their hungry families. Some of the food was the leavings of rich people. I remember a girl showing me the teeth marks of a baroness on a pork chop.

It was alright at the hospital until one night when me and the other girls broke out and squeezed ourselves through the bars. I still have dents on my breasts to this day. We went to a bar in the countryside where cows were tied up outside and the villagers danced about like pigs. I drank six green beers and was sick all over a young farmer. When we got home the matron caught us hanging off the drainpipes, and I got sacked for being the ringleader and bending hospital property.

All this time I read romantic books. I love books. I don't care what they're about, I just like the place they take me to. It's a room with big windows. When I was young the man who Ma slept with hated that room and would knock the book out of my hand. He even blew out the candles and the gaslight so I couldn't see, so half the time we grew up in the dark.

When I was fifteen I got disgusted with my Ma. She kept on having babies. They wouldn't stop coming out. I didn't agree with children then. All they did was eat. I liked the women in films who didn't have them; who lay about in floaty nighties and smoked in bed. I lost my temper with her and threw my keys at her man who dropped down unconscious. When he came round he was impotent.

He never spoke to me again, just wrote me orders on brown paper bags. There were no more babies.

I open my eyes. The stranger must have got lost. Ha Ha.

I feel as if everyone in my street is staring at me, and that something unusual is about to happen. I don't like it, my webby hands start to shake. I shut my eyes again and think.

When I was sixteen I started courting. I know for a fact that a lot of the boys were scared of me and hid when they saw me coming. I wasn't slow in coming forward even then. I judged a man by his mother. If she was slovenly, or over-loving, or mean, I knew he would be no good, and that the sparkle in his eyes was as temporary as  fairy lights from a market stall. Also I had a beautiful scarlet dress that I had handsewn myself, that was so silky it felt like running water in your fingers, and I didn't want it besmirched, so I was picky.

I was standing on the corner end waiting for a girlfriend when I met Billy. He came swaggering up and asked me for a kiss, so I hit him with my keys and cut him on the forehead. Later on he came round with a bandage on his head and asked me out to see Seventh Heaven at the Gaiety. That was more like it. The gas meter ran out when he was standing there and he gave my Ma a shilling and the lights went on for a long, long time and I confused this with love, or perhaps that's what love is, illumination.

Also, Billy told me his mother was a hairdresser, and an agoraphobic, and this worked in his favour.

He was a handsome man then. People thought he was foreign, because he'd been in India and he had dark skin and a jaunty moustache. His fingers were like a girl's, with delicate fingernails and thin wrists. It would have all been hunky dory if the army hadn't taken him off, and there hadn't been a war.

I'd hardly got to know him when he got sent to fight, and by the time he came back he was different. He had become a desert rat, and he had seen the insides of men's hearts strewn in the sand.

And he had lost his legs.

I would like to sue someone for what they did to Billy. I have written more letters than I care to count, but all you get back is regret letters.

We regret to say.

With our deepest regret.

Regretfully.

I hate that word.

One of my grandchildren bangs on the window pane and I open one eye. She looks like she's going to a party. She's wearing a pink dress with a bow at the back. I got her that dress . No one told me about any party. She is smiling at me and saying something about a surprise. Her mother comes running out and tugs her away, without even looking at me. A year ago I would have chased her down the street, but I'm tired. I don't even know how old I am anymore, I've lied about it so many times. I must be getting on. I was one of the older ones in the war when Billy was away.

I was a welder down at the shipyard. I've got scars round my eyes from the sparks. I built battleships. There was a whole lot of us. Women with flanks like horses and merciless wit. Most of them are dead now, or invisible. I see them sometimes in supermarkets, picking out the dented cans and pulling their hats down over their faces. I see them alright, but no bugger else does. We worked day and night, and never stopped until those ships steamed away up the river.

I reckon, after we got laid off, the whole enterprise went downhill. We even had to put on our own leaving do, with a couple of bottles of yellow gin off the black market. We had it in the engine room of a ship, and stripped off to our underwear and sang our heads off.

After we left the yards it was as if our time there was an embarrassment, because it was never mentioned. We had grown too big for our kitchens, and we couldn't work out how to be in them for a while. But I had a husband with no legs and that was that.

I couldn't have managed Billy if it hadn't been for his mother, Lotty, who lived a few miles up the hill. You see, Billy was mad.

A lot of men were mad. The women ignored it and just carried on, but after the war we were basically living in one great open air asylum, with no drugs to hand. If it hadn't been for the allotment society it would have been even worse.

Billy's madness was religious. He took up chanting, and would hobble down the street in a pair of orange calcutta pyjamas. After I had the children he made them chant too. Nobody said anything. they were too busy coping with husbands and fathers who thoughts they were birds, or that they were being followed, or that they were still in the trenches, or the desert. We formed all kinds of sewing groups, and jam-making societies just to get away from them. And we locked them in sheds in the garden, and I still say that no woman's life is her own without a shed and a stout pad-lock.

The men who went back to work were better off. They could hide in shadows of the shipyards and the mines, and the noise drowned their nightmares, but there was a time when if you walked the street at night  all you could hear was bad dreams, flying about like bombs over your head.

I am sure I can smell meat pies. Something's cooking. I don't like waiting, and I don't like silence. It reminds me of death.

When Billy's mother died I cried for a whole month, and you can still see the ditches down my cheeks from the tears.

Her hairdressing business was in her front room, and it was one of the safe places for a lot of women. Nothing bad could happen to you there. It smelt of ammonia and burnt plastic, and there was always biscuits and gossip, and women's business to sort out (and I'm not talking about recipe swapping, I'm talking life and death). Lotty gave me free perms and rinses, and if Billy was bad all I had to do was wave a hair roller at him to shut him up.

When Lotty died we found her sat in the salon with a woman's magazine on her lap with an article in it on "How To Deal With Bereavement". Even in death she was considerate. At the church the pews were filled with women whose hair had been tamed by her clever fingers, and I couldn't help wondering what would happen to the appearance of the area now she had gone. I for one went downhill, and never got the hang of home rinses.

The stranger turns the corner. I can see him clearly now. He walks along my street, looking at the doors one by one. I squeeze my keys.

As he strolls along all my family start stepping out of the houses and standing on the pavement.

There's a lot of laughter in the air. I feel left out.

The stranger rings the doorbell. I slowly walk to the door.

"Yes," I say. Stern. I built battleships.

"Are you Mrs Steel?"

I look beyond his cardboard features to the crowd of relatives who have gathered outside. My daughters are smiling and nodding their heads. Is it my birthday?

"Congratulations," he smiles.

"What's going on?" I bellow. I am getting really mad. The bull in me is showing the whites of its eyes.

"You've lived here all your life haven't you?" A camera flashes.

"Watch it!" I snort. My keys are in my fist.

"And this is your family?"

I step backwards.

"We have a surprise for you."

I take a swing at him. He tumbles backwards. Unfortunately I miss his head. He lies on the rosebeds shaking his bureaucratic head, and a dog licks his ear.

"What is it?" I say abruptly.

At this my eldest daughter steps out holding what looks like a plank under her arm. She holds it up. I squint. My eyes aren't good and a sudden ray of sunshine obscures my vision. Then I see it. It's a fucking street sign, and it's my name. They are going to name the street after me. Amy Street.

A lot of thoughts flash through my head then. People say before they die they see their lives, like a film, flashing in front of them. Everyone was waiting for me to be pleased, and to be polite.

But one thing I don't have in my blood is gratefulness. I take the sign. I look at it without smiling and then frown into the eyes of the local press photographer who waits for a sweet old granny to brush the tears from her eyes.

I think, "Is this the prize at the end? Is this all? A bloody sign."

The stranger knows he isn't wanted. He staggers to his feet, and mutters something aggressive in my daughter's ear, then stamps off down Amy Street looking for his lost face.

The ceremony ends awkwardly.

But when they've gone, and I see my people standing in the street, looking disappointed, I stamp my foot and let a smile winch up the corners of my mouth. It's about time, I thought. About time a woman left her bloody mark.

And then we have a party, and I get mortal drunk and tell them the story of my life.

# Lilo

It is a hot day in winter. We are all there, on the beach, in a steep seaside place. There are two small boys in the family, with thin arms and sharp wet legs; a father with a porous nose; a flawed and impatient mother; and a girl with a mottled hairless skin , wearing a puckered bathing costume with a limp pink bow. I am the girl. There is a Swedish au pair called Oona with bleached hair and a white bikini that fits her body like a sealskin. Father is reading an almanac and fingering a corned beef sandwich. He is stuck in a deckchair. He won't take off his shoes. He says he must go somewhere soon.

Mother has nested beyond a breakwater. She is reading the obituaries in The Times, and her hair is contained in a daunting black scarf, which makes her a landmark, even though she tries to be unnoticeable. Around her feet her two small sons, my brothers, ferret in the sand, throwing up grainy storms with tin spades. The sand is black and their puny limbs are bruised with it. Mother orders them off and fingers an Embassy cigarette in the bottom of her beach bag. It's common to smoke outside.

There is a third boy in the family whose brain is too big for his head. He is constructing an oil rig from lollipop sticks. You would only know he was part of this family by the way he pretends not to know them. His name is Frank. He will become a household name, by performing dubious miracles in public places, such as moving clouds in the sky or appropriating objects from people's handbags, but now he is just a pubescent boy, building an oil rig.

Oona knows how to sunbathe. It's in her genes. She lies on a lilo behind a frontier of suntan lotions and has a gadget; a pulpy plastic envelope that lies heavily over her eyes. We want the lilo. It belongs to us, and Oona has plumped herself on it. Mother glances at her with contempt. None of the girls she procures knows how to clean a lavatory. They all get homesick, and only pretend to love children in letters. I amble about, looking at Oona, looking at mother. I twist one of the boy's ears and spit at the other. I sidle up to Frank, who turns his acnied back to me. I slope back to Oona and tap her firm, greasy thigh. She takes off her eye cover and scowls. I try to explain the word SWIMMING to her, using arm movements. I point at the lilo and then to the bow on my chest. Oona shakes her head. Mother is asleep now, and the newspaper is blowing in wheels along the beach.

I start all over again with Oona, who wipes her arms with white cream, then gets up when I am mid-stroke, picks up the lilo, and lollops down to the calmish sea. She launches herself into the shallows and lies face up with her arms drooping languidly over the sides. It's all very quiet. Father's deckchair is empty; a seagull carries the remains of his corned beef sandwich high up in the sky. Mother is in the fathoms of slumber. I bury my leg in the sand, until it feels numb and dislocated from the rest of my body. I imagine that I am a one-legged person and wait for a kind passer-by to feel sorry on my behalf. Hours pass.

Then one of the small boys sees an orange cruise-liner sliding along the top edge of the sea; like a ship in a novelty pen. The boys all get up and shout and wave, as if we are shipwrecked, desperate to be heard. I wrench my dead limb from its cold grave and limp hopefully down to the sea. Soon there is an almighty wash and vast booming waves are crashing along the shoreline. We applaud, as if it's a passing parade, and run about in the froth.

Then, gradually, the wash slips back to nothing. That's when Frank speaks.

"Where is Oona?" says Frank slowly.

We crane our necks and fan our eyes.

Frank shrugs and picks up a pebble in the shape of a heart.

I tug at mother's black headscarf and she slaps my hand viciously and wakes up. One of the boys screams very piercingly:

"Where's our lilo?!"

One side of mother's face is red and creased from where it has pressed against the breakwater. She is so angry that she pulls her cigarette out of the bag and lights it, trembling still from a nightmare about a number thirty-one bus.

"What?" she snarls. She does look common.

"Oona's floated off on our lilo," bleat the small boys in squeaking unison.

"For God's sake!"

The tide has seeped away now. The family are a long way from anything. From the promenade we are a little clump of people alone in a daunting expanse.

Mother stands up and shrieks. Even the youths in the penny arcade hear her, and the seaside town turns its head. She runs, still shrieking, towards the pier. Frank tries to roll himself into an invisible ball as she passes, but she still kicks him. The small boys cry and hunch their shoulders. I run through the dipping rockpools calling... "Ooonaaa, Oooonaaa!"

I sound like a sea-bird. I am nearly hoarse.

"Ooooooonaaaaaa!!"

It starts to snow.

On the quayside there is a dull bang and a flare whooshes above us. We cheer. A posse of men in yellow plastic anoraks gallop out of nowhere, crushing Frank's oil rig with big leathery wellington boots. They carry an inflatable lifeboat, and disappear into the sea after Oona.

Father comes back. His breath smells fruity and he has mislaid his almanac. He squints at the horizon and shrugs. Mother puts on his large flecked sweater and walks up and down like a hungry dog. She tells father to take us home, but he shakes his big head. When mother is like this it is better to do nothing.

When the men return, some hours later, and the sun has quite gone, and the sea purrs, and the family is a line of cold people wrapped in wet towels who wait, they bring back the deflated lilo. One of the men holds it up, as if it is a skin.

"He's got the lilo!" chirrup the boys happily.

Father intones the Lord's Prayer, then he tiptoes off to the police station.

At home we eat fishfingers.

I ask mother, as she scours the frying pan:

"Where is Sweden?"

"Look in the atlas," she snaps and blows her nose on a dishcloth.

I go upstairs to the cabinet where the encyclopaedias are kept. Bits of Oona are all over the house; mascara in the bathroom; a white leathery coat hangs over the bannister; Swedish postcards propped on the mantelpiece. Oona's bedroom door is open; it smells of wet bathing costumes in there, but I don't go in.

I look at the green map of Sweden; its head hung over the Baltic Sea. Like Oona, it is just a shape.

Frank is mending the lilo with a bicycle repair kit.

The next day mother goes to town on the thirty-one bus with a face like a church. My father takes us to a tea-room where there are cakes as big as pillows. We each drink a milkshake with a long straw and look up mournfully at the waitress. When the glasses are empty we sit there with nothing to do, waiting for mother to come. After a while the waitress taps her watch and counts the coins in the till.

"Where is mother?" says Frank.

# Jordan With Poppies

There is the picture. It is a shock, seeing it here, and I am embarrassed. Renate has walked away, her silk scarf trailing behind her. Her friends are in the other gallery. She is not interested in paint; she says it is nostalgic. Through the cool white rooms I can hear her voice as she talks. She sounds like a radio play. Renate and I are not speaking today. I have spent the morning looking up at rooftops and avoiding her eyes. She makes me behave like an adolescent.

I make myself look again at the picture. My face, my body look back at me. I look around the room; half expecting to see her here, standing near her work, nervously presenting it to me.

Her shyness was in her eyes.

I used to write poems about her. I had never met anyone like her before and the feeling was a harvest that lasted for only one summer. I don't know what I would think about her now. Then my life experience was quite limited. I was more or less a child. I still had posters stuck with sellotape to my bedroom walls, and believed I could change the shape of my nose by sleeping with a peg clinched round my nostrils.

And I still wished for things if a black cat crossed my path.

I met her in a field. At that time my uncle employed me to pick the bright poppies from his cornfields. I got paid depending on his mood. The poppies poison the corn, however picturesque they may look. They were bitter and acrid, and the hairy stalks made my hands raw.

I was standing with a handful of poppies in the centre of a yellow field when I saw a woman drawing with an easel in front of her some distance away. She looked up and waved. As I didn't know her I just trudged on down the line, getting gradually closer to where she was sitting. I considered ducking down into the forest of stalks and disappearing into the hedge, but you never know where you might pop up, so I just carried on wrenching the flowers out of the soil and getting gradually closer to her.

When I got nearer I could see her looking at me, frowning, then looking back at her drawing. She was about the same age as my mother, but entirely different. She had skin like chamois leather; my mother's was more like suet.

Then she called over to me. She wanted to know if I kept the poppies and I said no, I just piled them up in smelly heaps. She asked if she could have a bunch, to put in water, and I said yes and gave her a handful, although I could see that the petals were dropping off already.

She stood up and we looked at each other awkwardly. She asked me if I knew her husband, and I said I didn't.

"Well, he's dead anyway," she said, and laughed, although her expression was tangled. Then she asked me if I wanted to come back to her house for a cup of black tea, as she had no milk. I had seen her house before; it was behind the four trees that had survived the endless fields; four trees that stood out starkly on the skyline between one sea of corn and another. Her house tottered on an uneven ridge. The walls were grey with old whitewash, and there was an old tea towel flapping on the washing line. My uncle had told me that it was full of hippies who left rubbish lying about and pretended to live off the land. As we walked silently up the weedy garden path I couldn't see any sign of cultivation, only a rusty pram that lay in a patch of nettles.

Inside it was more like a garage. There were paintings stacked up against the walls and not much furniture. A pool of sunlight spotlit a row of paint pots, covered in fingerprints and standing in a sticky puddle of spilt paint. I didn't know where to sit, so I just stood in the middle of the room, blushing.

She told me her name was Anne and made some tea in a pot with no handle and stirred it with a spoon. The cups were smeared with oil paint too and the rim tasted of turpentine.

"Sit down," she said and pointed to an armchair in the corner of the room.

"Are they your paintings?" I asked uneasily, wishing I was somewhere else.

"No, his."

She went on after a difficult silence:

"He was very difficult to live with. He drank. He was quite well known really."

"What did he paint?"

"Me." She turned one of the canvases round. It was a nude. The whole painting was one rough, fleshy body, with no head.

"Do you like them?" She kept turning more pictures round until the whole room was full of thighs and breasts, contorted and brash. Some of them had her face staring out at me; recognisable although abstracted to shadow and colour.

"I don't know," I answered truthfully.

"I don't."

"Were you cold?"

"Sometimes. We had an electric heater. I was bored though, very bored."

"Oh."

The tea had been drunk. She placed the poppies in a blue vase on the floor. I had never really looked at them before and they suddenly seemed graceful and quiet.

I stood up.

"I'm trying to paint myself. I used to, but then I stopped. You wouldn't model for me would you?"

She stood in the doorway looking at me.

"Naked?"

"It doesn't matter. It could just be a portrait. You've got an interesting face. I'll pay you."

"I'd better not."

My face was vermilion. I gave her my cup and she stepped out of my way. I could hardly say goodbye. I ran home as fast as I could.

That night I stood on a chair in front of the bathroom mirror and looked at my body. It was like a stalk. I had big elbows and knees. My spine was knobbled, and my breasts were quite lost in a complicated pattern of oversize bones. No one had ever taken an interest in it.

I changed my mind.

When I called round the next day she was lying in bed. The door was open and she called me up the stairs. Her bedroom was as bare as the room downstairs. She was sitting in bed eating a bowl of cornflakes, looking small and delicate in a pile of dirty blankets. Her sleepy face was even more leathery and taut than the day before and her eyes were black and coaly. Her fingers were bruised with smudges of paint.

"I'll model for you," I whispered.

"Good." She grinned broadly at me.

We arranged for me to go round every day, after pulling up poppies. There was nothing more to say after that, so I retreated back down the stairs. She was the first adult I had ever met who had no social grace. I was hooked.

The next morning I washed very carefully and sprayed my armpits with deodorant. I was afraid that my adolescence would smell. My mother was frying my breakfast. She had pink furry slippers on and her voice was soft as a dumpling. The kitchen looked like a picture in a magazine. I despised its cleanliness.

I asked my mother about the house between the fields and she shook her soft head and clucked disapprovingly.

"He was nasty, the husband. I saw him sometimes, staggering down the lane, chuntering to himself. He died of whisky."

She looked up from her shopping list.

"And?"

"As far as I know he wasn't very nice to his wife either. They said he was famous in New York and places like that, but so what? Why?"

She looked at me curiously.

"Nothing," I said quickly "I was just looking at the house, that's all."

That summer I went from ripping up poppies to reclining half naked on a mildewed sofa in her front room. At night I wrote poetry. My mother describes that time as my most difficult phase. I certainly stopped speaking. Nothing ever changed in Anne's house. Things rotted before you. All summer I watched the bunch of poppies decaying in the blue vase; wilting, then sagging until they were a spidery mass of dried out pods and sticks.

She finished four paintings of me. One was a portrait in which I was startled like a rabbit with a torch shone in its eyes; another was a painting of my naked back and face in profile; the third was of me in a blue shirt drinking tea; and the last, which hangs before me now was a full-length portrait. I am lying on the sofa. The poppies are dying beside me.

When the summer ended my uncle set fire to the stubble and for days the air hung with smouldering smoke. I helped Anne move her husband's paintings into an outhouse and in their place she stacked the ones of me.

Then she kissed me, lightly on the cheek and said:

"Thankyou."

"That's alright," I said.

"No really. It's been worth it. It was hard starting again, after all that."

The four trees were nearly bare and the teatowel flapped in the autumn wind. She pressed some money into my hand.

"It's O.K," I said.

"Have it. It was an agreement."

I took the money. I spent it on oil paint.

Renate was calling my name. I looked at the painting once more. Below it was the title 'JORDAN WITH POPPIES'.

I walked out of the gallery. Renate sat on the steps looking bad-tempered. Her friends had gone.

"What's the matter with you now?" she snapped.

We went to a coffee bar by the river, and ordered cappucinos. I smiled at Renate who frowned back, puzzled by my change of heart.

Then I chucked her; quickly and without ceremony. She gasped and looked as if she might shout, but then didn't. She just shrugged and nodded, stood up and wound her bright scarf neatly around her neck, and walked off.

And now I just want things to be quiet for a while. I am going to watch and listen.

I am not going to analyse or struggle.

I am just going to sit here, in this cafe, as it gets dark, watching the street lights go on across the river as the cold red sun sets...

# Running

Today I am going to make a decision about my future. I have been working up to it.

I run to the top of a cold hill in a pair of red and white shorts. As I run, flocks of young women pushing buggies laden heavily with bags and wide-eyed babies walk past me. They look like people on film; brightly-coloured and plastic. Some of the women wave. I know them from school. There are girls who have half-throttled me in the dingy shadows of the playground, and girls who I have practised French kissing with until our lips were red and sore. Now their lips move with the ease of tired mothers, their shoulders slope downwards, and they have bags full of purses and scraps of paper.

I wonder if they remember those kisses?

They are on their way down to the old town like a flock of birds, to see their mothers, to spend the day in a clutter of milky bottles and carrier bags. They have a language, these young women, that only their mothers understand. It has never been written down. It is full of tuts and sniffs.

I have no babies, and no mother. Something in their eyes says 'poor little Ange', and makes me feel homesick in the back of my throat. I fight it back, this feeling of exclusion, and remember that I am descended from a woman who shot a lion that had escaped from a nearby zoo. The lion is stuffed and moth-eaten in the municipal gallery, but it has my great-grandmother's name embossed beneath its front claws. My family has class.

I run past seedy single men, walking slowly with leadless dogs. Although I know some of them, running is an antidote to conversation. No one talks to runners. The men stop, smoke, look up at the sky and wander on; past the river bank with its great signs announcing enterprise and development, fronting the mud hills and prefabricated huts . What do men think about when they walk with their dogs? My Nana, Bella, said they all had machinery going hammer and tongs in their heads, which is why they often don't seem to be really  all there. She had a lot of theories like that. She died when I was six. She was complaining about a mince pie that , she said, tasted as if someone had cried bitter tears into it, when she choked  and fell down flat in the middle of her street.

Auntie Stanley says the men are thinking about sex. Over and over again. Then she prunes a shoot off a plant with one swipe of her secateurs. The year is 1994. I am seventeen. I have grown up watching my sisters and my friends have babies. My family is slopping over the brim of this Northern city.  It is so huge that you wouldn't know if you were going out with your own half-brother.

Right now I'm in turmoil because I can't decide what to do, which is why I keep running. I've been running round and round the paths and hills and alleys and back lanes and building sites and wastelands of this town.  Thinking.

My new friend Susan wants me to go away with her.

Maybe I will, maybe I won't.

My old friend Mary wants me to stay.

Maybe I will, maybe I won't.

When I was young I collected tickets. I loved the feeling of tickets. I papered my bedroom with them. Buses, boats, planes, anything.  I had travel in my blood and one day I believed that, like a great ship, I would slide out of the shipyards into the great blue green and yellow world that was in the atlases.

But now I'm frightened.  Short-circuited by anxiety. I can't stop running to try and keep my hair from standing on end.

Susan wants me to go down to London with her and share a

flat. That word, FLAT, always makes me think of a sardine can. I keep seeing London like a great dark fishy pit. I dream about it. Getting mangled up in it.

But why would I want to stay here?

Auntie Stanley is one reason. I love Auntie Stanley. She is Bella's youngest sister and she has fingers as green as grass snakes. I live with her, and even though she would never say so, she needs me.

I've been living with Auntie Stanley since my dad was killed in an accident at the yards and mother admitted herself to a hospital, because she said she couldn't think straight anymore. I am always worried not thinking straight might be in my genes. I try not to run in circles. When I am afraid I think of lions.

Auntie Stanley has gradually pruned me and encouraged me and re-potted me until I am a young healthy plant. When she got me I was a limp yellow stalk.

Another reason I want to stay here is the map in my head. Here I know the safe places and the dangerous ones. I know the routes from one house to another. I can look after myself, and because of that I can laugh and relax. I can hold my head up. What would happen to me in London, without a map? I would drown in the high buildings and run out of air in the underground .

People say Northern women are hard. Perhaps they are, but I would use another word. I would say they were shrewd. That they know their patch and make maximum use of every possible inch of it. Northern women are dredgers, that sieve the bottom of the river.

People say I have been an old woman ever since I was a baby.

I stop for air. Far to my right is the cool oblong of a Japanese car factory; its soundless carcasses of cars hanging from butchers hooks. Ahead is the empty river, steady and brown in the centre of its changing banks, and to my left the necklaces of houses flung down the hillside. This town has a huge sky. A sky like a great sheet, and the more they change the landscape the bigger the sky gets. Sometimes it feels like a shroud.

Who am I?

I feel as if I've got no pins attaching me to anything. Babies are pins. All my friends have babies now. Big babies, little babies, pink ones and blue ones. Auntie Stanley is my pin. A safety pin.

She is an oasis.

Auntie Stanley is gardening mad.  She grows things from cuttings she gets from other peoples' gardens. She roams stately homes and hedgerows with her secateurs and carrier bag. Our council house is filled with seed trays and we eat our supper off gardening manuals because there is no room for a plate on the kitchen table. She's fond of climbers...sweet william and honey-suckle, and wild rose. She trains their curling stems around the yard. When the sun is out we sit in deckchairs and listen to them growing.

Outside our house the whole estate is being hacked about. Some of the houses have new front doors, like women with nose jobs. Everyone is after  government money.  It's as hard to catch as thistledown.

We are always being watched. On the estates flocks of camera crews come to ask us about our Depression. We are used to their sympathetic lenses. We know what they want. Government minis-ters drive along the streets in black cars, shaking their heads as they pass graffiti. Most of the improvements come in the form of signs that tell us of things that. are intended. ON THIS SITE THERE WILL BE A LEISURE COMPLEX. The signs are new and high, so that they cannot be desecrated. ON THIS SHITE.

All this change is confusing. All the old landmarks are going. Places I used to play when I was a kid aren't there anymore. All the clocks have stopped in the town. Some don't even have any hands.

Susan is a new friend. I met her at the gym. She has a pony tail and her dad is a white collar worker at the Japanese plant. She is a new brand of person. I didn't go to school with her and the thing we have in common is sport. To her North is just a passing-through place. She never knew it when it breathed and smoked and belched.

I took her to the museum once. She was not impressed by the lion in the museum, and bought postcards of cats instead.

Susan is confident more or less anywhere.

Yesterday we went running down on the river path, with the mud sticking to our shoes. She always runs in front and I jog along behind. She takes the mickey out of me, but she likes me. She says I'm her only friend.

Auntie Stanley says her roots would never grow in this soil, and I look at my feet and wonder if they are like Susan's. What's the soil like in London, I think?

But we're different. We look at the world through different windows. Like yesterday when we ran past a group of men in dayglo anoraks digging up the road, and they whistled at us. Susan stuck her fingers up, but half of the men were my uncles and cousins so I just waved. That's the difference between us.

We go to the wine bars down by the river that smell of putty and damp, and drink white wine and soda. Men try and pick us up sometimes. They lurk around us and buy us drinks. They're men I've never seen before. Men with watches, conditioned hair, and polished shoes. I slept with one once, but his aftershave made me feel giddy and I'd never do it again. It was just curiosity. I wanted to see what he was like underneath, but I never found out because I kept my eyes closed. His skin felt like wax. I didn't tell Susan about it.

I told Mary. Mary is my oldest friend. I know her body as well as my own. She was the girl I kissed most. When we were at school she had a laugh like a dog barking, and she couldn't stop writing her name everywhere; on the walls, on the blackboard, even on her arms. Mary just laughed about the man and made me tell her again. She loves talking about sex. She puts her big mouth right near my ear and whispers sexual secrets so loudly that they fill my head for days.

I reckon she was hoping I'd get pregnant, but I'm not stupid. I'm clever. That's the problem.

Then I told Mary I might be going to London with Susan and she stopped laughing and her eyes went hard as steel and she turned her back on me and changed the baby's nappy.

I asked her what was the matter; I said I would probably come back anyway.

"Oh yeah," she said. "But you won't be the same will you!"

That's when I realised there was no room for experiments.

So today is decision time. Susan wants me to go to London. I haven't got a job, and I haven't got a baby. All I've got is a city of relations, and no chance of a job, and a drawerful of college prospectuses.

It starts to rain. The drops are plump and depressed. A businesswoman in a smart car drives past and splashes my legs. A gang of cleaners under one umbrella pass me. I can hear them whispering and joking with their heads close together as if they are one person. One of them murmurs as they pass, "Get those wet clothes off little Ange, and stop worrying," then they giggle a bit more.

That's what it's like living here. People know what you're thinking. I know what they're thinking too. If I went away I would cut off those inner lines of communication. Between the women, that is. As I said, who knows what the men think.

I am so wet that I try to get wetter. My legs are covered with watery shapes like maps. I imagine I am running away, but inside I know whichever way I turn I'll end up back home with Auntie Stanley grinning at me with earth smeared down her cheeks.

She makes her own world, and it's a jungle.

Later on I am sitting on the settee in my dressing gown. Auntie Stanley is crocheting a red and white doll with boggle eyes for a raffle. She says:

"Made your mind up yet Ange?"

I look at her. Her legs are soft and wide, her fingernails are encrusted with earth. She's wearing a poncho she bought at a Women's Legion Coffee Morning. Her smile is sweet as a lolli-pop.

"Did you never want to leave?" I ask, picking red shiny threads from a nearby cushion.

"I went to London," Auntie Stanley said. "I ran away with a runaway miner. We slept in a botanical garden, in a greenhouse, under a cactus that breathed. It was alright."

"Why did you come back?"

"The miner got homesick. The headlights got in his eyes, so I came home with him. He said I was too flighty. How far can you run these days?" she asks, casually.

"Don't know," I say, gloomily.

"Why don't you see how far you can run? Run away."

Then she gets up and sits the ridiculous doll on the mantelpiece, and turns off the television, which is one of her irritating habits, and goes to bed. So I'm left stuck in silence being stared at.

My legs ache. I open the back door and the yard rustles with leaves. A baby is screaming somewhere down the street.

See how far I can run. I can run further than anyone I know. I am weightless, even though I am just Little Ange. Nothing can catch me; I have no buggies to push, no door to lock.

And somewhere beyond the muddy river a lion is roaring.

# Bridge

"Concentrate!"

I look at the red and black cards on the green baize. They are full of trickery and promise. I know this even though I am only eight.

Aunt Adele is drumming her long pink nails on the pad of paper next to her. The room is cobweb red, and the table is in the centre. Three other women sit around the green table. They are good-humoured. Each has a brooch pinned to her breast. Alice has a rose, Maria has a bird, and Edna has an encrusted eye. Aunt Adele is not jolly. She is playing three no trumps. Maria and Edna are playing four hearts. We are in the front room of a small terraced house.

This room is a card house. It is quiet as a clock. There is a picture on each wall of a woman with a low-cut dress on, showing peachy breasts. I look at each picture in turn. The curtains are drawn. I have an Enid Blyton book on my knee, but I don't read it. I am too scared. I just concentrate on the game, as we all must.

Aunt Adele is the queen, and Alice is her partner, although she is more of a handmaid. Her hands tremble very slightly, even though she is only the Dummy.

My mother has left me here for the weekend. She said she wanted to have a rest. She tried several other people first, but none would have me. Aunt Adele was grudging, but said she would come for Christmas in return. My mother sighed and nodded. It was a last resort.

Aunt Adele lives in a street behind a motorway. Even the trees are breathless. She smokes cocktail cigarettes, and drinks small sherries, and shops in Fenwick's Fine Foods.

She isn't married, and she doesn't seem to work, but she isn't poor. She has people round to play cards, and sometimes men take her out. Once she went on a cruise, and sent me a postcard of the Queen.

She is not interested in children. She doesn't like me to speak, but she doesn't like me to be silent either. I don't know what she wants. Sometimes we go to the park. Sometimes I take her dog, Jack, for a walk around the block. Sometimes I watch television; or Aunt makes an effort and shows me card tricks.

During the bridge game Adele's mouth is a long thin line. I haven't spoken for over an hour. I sit on the edge of the room, listening to the murmurs of the bridge players. My aunt has so much blue eye-shadow on that her eyes keep shutting.  She wears a large purple ring on her index finger that reflects the light.

When the evening is over the other players leave pleasantly, kissing Adele on the cheek, and thanking her for the game.  My aunt sweeps up the packs of cards in her dead fingers and looks at me triumphantly.

"I won," she snaps.

Aunt Adele is hard and metallic, like an old silver tea-set.

"Tomorrow," she says, "you can learn how to play Patience."

Tomorrow is a bleak pool I must swim across. I slip out of the room and go and brush my teeth. I can hear my aunt talking to herself downstairs; going through bids, snapping card-boxes shut.

The rest of her house is a mess. Drawers spill with torn paper, the kitchen is full of grease, the toilet has a brown stain, my sheets are old and yellow. The only other room which is nice is her bedroom, which has frilly curtains and a dressing table with hundreds of brushes and pots and feathers.

When my mother comes to collect me she is thinner and her hair is lank. She thanks Aunt Adele over-profusely and gives her a huge box of chocolates. Aunt Adele gives me an embroidered handkerchief in a square packet. I curtsy and mother laughs, but Aunt Adele bows her head as if I have behaved appropriately.

When I get home I find a pack of cards and pick out the royals.

"Why does Aunt Adele want to win so badly?" I ask mother as she picks her way around me wearily with a brush in her hand.

"I don't know," my mother says, straightening her back. "She is just that kind of person." I have a feeling that my mother is lying. It's got something to do with the way she stares at her brush.

"What does she live on?"

"Freja, I don't know. Nobody knows."

I am nine when Adele comes for Christmas. There is me; a man with a beard, who I have just met, called Larry; Mother and Adele. We sit uneasily around the carcass of a turkey, and I start thinking about dead birds. I excuse myself and go and play patience in the parlour.

I can hear Aunt Adele chewing her sprouts. Larry has a loud voice that matches the Christmas crackers. My paper hat is giving me a headache.

After dinner they all loll about in armchairs, apart from Adele who sits upright, playing with her rings.

"How about a rubber?" she says, and Larry smirks as if it is a rude joke.

"I don't know if I remember how to play," says mother, who would rather watch *Gone With The Wind*.

"Freja knows how to play," says my Aunt, defiantly.

"I'll give you a game!" Larry rubs his hairy hands together as if he is about to play tennis.

"Good." Aunt Adele swoops into her handbag and unwraps the cellophane from a new pack of cards, then shuffles them, her nails clicking on the table.

"You can be my partner, Freja."

We sit around a small coffee table. At first it is light-hearted, but as the afternoon darkens and our dinners settle, the game gets grim and more deathly. Every time Larry or my mother makes a move Adele raises her painted eyebrows in disgust, or whistles through her teeth with a grimace. When it's my turn to play I feel a stiletto shoe needling my shins. Later I notice my lower legs are covered in bruises the size of sixpences.

We win.

Larry is annoyed and gets himself a whisky. Mother says:

"Oh Larry, put some music on," in an attempt to lighten the heaviness of defeat. Adele plays with the cards; spreading them over the table and gloating.

Larry puts a Beatles record on. *A Hard Day's Night.*

Mother says, "Not pop music," and stares hard at Larry, but he doesn't get up from his chair.

"Change the music Larry!" Aunt Adele says without looking at him.

He obeys her sheepishly.

"Why don't we play rummy?" I say.

Aunt looks up at me crossly.

"I don't play any other games. I only play bridge," she snaps.

I get my new jigsaw out then and Larry tries to help me. I wish he would go home.

When I am fifteen I discover Adele's profession. It is Easter, and Mother and I visit, leaving Larry watching *This Is Your Life* on the television. We knock on the door carrying a bunch of sour-smelling daffodils. It is meant to be a surprise. Alice looks through the letter-box, then unbolts the door.

The house smells of violets and alcohol. We stand in the dark hallway, feeling awkward. Alice says our names very loudly, then tells us that Adele is ill.

Then a man comes down the stairs and brushes past us without speaking.

Alice looks guilty.

Adele appears at the top of the stairs in a black dressing gown.
"You should have called," she says. "I'm not ready."

It is a short and embarrassing visit.

Adele is on the game.

I am thirty years old. I am a vegetarian, and a feminist. Mother is married to Larry, and they argue all the time. They argue about money and drink. Aunt Adele is dying of cancer. She is riddled with it. I imagine it as a kind of fungus growing all over her body. I blame men. Mother has been looking after her, but she just does it out of duty. She goes to see her every Saturday and washes the sheets. I say to my mother:

"She's got a nurse hasn't she?" I have become quite hard lately. It's because I teach personal skills in a comprehensive school, and I deal with children who are unable to concentrate, even if I am talking about orgasms, or condoms, or venereal disease.

Then Mother asks me to go and see Aunt Adele. She says that her and Larry are going to stay in a hotel on the south coast to talk about separation. Perhaps it's the thought of no more Larry that makes me say yes.

I have quite forgotten Aunt Adele.

When I arrive at the house, after a long train journey opposite a man with an ill-fitting tie who winks at me every time I look up, it seems as if the motorway has swelled, and Aunt Adele's house has shrunk and withered. The aged street lights flicker on and off, and Home Helps click down the pavement. Old ladies' faces peer out from behind frosted glass. There is a smell of iodine and Dettol in the foggy atmosphere.

A Caribbean nurse answers the door with a grateful smile. She has her coat on as if she has been longing for me to arrive.

"Your aunt is upstairs," she says quickly as she runs down the path. I feel in my bag for the bottle of vodka I have brought with me. It is going to be a difficult weekend. I wish I was somewhere else.

Inside it is extraordinarily clean; as if each room has been fumigated of immorality and baptised by well-trained hospital staff. The kitchen is scrubbed down, the stairs are hoovered.

I hear a weak call from the bedroom and get two glasses and tiptoe upstairs. I wonder why we are always timid in the presence of the sick?

I expected her to be in bed, but she is fully dressed, in a black evening dress, sitting waiting for me.

She is wearing haphazard make-up, and her rings lie jangling loosely on her thin fingers. She has shrunk to the size of a small nut. Her face is brown and beady, and her shoulders are two tiny twigs.

"Has she gone?" she says.

"Yes. Hallo."

I bend down to kiss her, but she brushes me away.

"No time for that," she grunts. "Get me downstairs."

"Are you sure?" I ask.

"Yes."

We lurch downstairs. I know where we're going. She feels like a bag of wishbones. Together we hobble into the front room.

"There!" She points to the chair. I lever her into it.

"Turn the heating up."

The room is hot, but I do what she says.

"They've even been in here," she growls. I stand there wondering what to do, then remember the vodka.

"Thank God," she mutters, as I pour us a vodka each.

"They've ruined all my things," she says.

"It's very tidy down here."

"I know." Aunt Adele wheezes into her glass. I silently hope that she won't die on me. I am rather squeamish.

"I'm not finished yet, Freja," she whispers.

Who is Aunt Adele? I look into her glittering eyes. They are black aces, hell-bent on winning.

The doorbell rings. My aunt struggles up

"I'll get it."

"No!" And she staggers to the door, opens it, and there stand Edna, Maria and Alice, smiling querulously and smacking their gums. They see me, standing behind my aunt ready to catch her and squeal.

"Little Freja!"

As they nip my cheeks I notice my aunt swaying and quickly motion them into the card room.

Then they play bridge.

The game is as tense as ever, and there is no small talk, just bidding, nodding, the snap of a cigarette lighter, the low cough of the terminally ill.

Alice, Edna and Maria are so old that they look like angels.

Adele is still a devil.

She wins.

Her victory brings a small flush of pleasure to her cheeks. Then she motions for me to take her upstairs. The three ladies wave from the stairwell, calling:

"Next week, same time, same place!" as we drag our way back up to bed. Once there I offer to undress her but she shakes her head. It occurs to me that maybe she sleeps in her black dress.

As I turn to leave her she says:

"I want you to have this," and gives me the fat purple ring I once watched as a child.

"Thanks." I slip it onto my finger. It looks ridiculous, but I shall wear it all the same.

Downstairs I hear crying coming from the kitchen and find Alice sitting at the table with a handkerchief clenched to her nose.

"What is it Alice?"

"It's Adele. She's such a wonderful person."

I squeeze her thin arm and make her some sweet tea.

"We're so lucky, to have known her."

I sit down and nod.

"She won't last much longer."

"Will that be the end of the game then?" I ask sympathetically.

"Yes, I suppose it will." Alice sniffs into her tea. "No one could take her place."

And I suppose no one could.

"Don't you get tired of her winning all the time?" I asked quietly. Alice looks up at me white-faced.

"No," she says. "Never. I love her."


The funeral is at a blackened chapel with rows of families waiting outside, like a bus queue.

There is a crowd of women with dyed black hair and red lips. I sit at the front with Mother, who has left Larry.

Edna, Maria and Alice sit on the other side.

Afterwards we stand beside the grave. The light makes the grass lurid green.

As the vicar mutters his last words, Alice throws a pack of cards down onto the coffin. They flutter and fall gracefully onto the dark cheap wood.

# Waving At The Queen

Her whitish lips crumpled and she sighed in a voice as limp as my legs:

"You know I really loved him."

I had an impulse to reach down her throat, pull her heart up and out of her body, and to examine its structure, its strange mutations. It was green, I decided, and mildewed.

"I loved him," she intoned again, sitting on a sofa-bed with her moist spongy face looking pious.

There was no point disagreeing. Della doesn't like conflict. She prefers dreaming. Sometimes I would like to punch her, to wake her up. The punches would never reach her. I am marooned in a wheelchair. My legs are deflated and shrivelled.

In front of us, on the floral carpet, there was a dark patch; a pool of shadow. I thought about stains then, about salt and cold water, egg white and brillo pads.

Della winced. Then she vomited. Then she smoked. Her skin was mottled and patchy. She was a bruise. She can be beautiful; when the lights are right, and her collar is ironed.

We went to the morgue. I was hoping that there would be the usual access problems, and that I would be abandoned in the car park. Instead we found a lift that descended gracefully into the cool catacombs designed for the recently dead. I expected an attendant with a white coat to chaperone us, and we would be meek and mumble:

"Yes, that's him," and Della would sniff into a small embroidered handkerchief. We would have sweet tea afterwards and I would pat her bowed head.

It wasn't like that. We were shown by a young, sunburnt boy

into a medicinal square room. He left us all alone, with Fred Hams, on the slab, harmless at last.

Fred Hams was Della's common law husband. Fred Hams called me Della's 'crip' sister, and believed that people like me should be put down. Here he was, lying like some embalmed saint; his marshy brain quite empty, his fluids drained, his big fists limp and gentle, and his bitter tongue obedient and servile.

I would have drunk a bottle of best Brut over his still chest, but Della's grief filled the room, like gas.

"Isn't he handsome?" she whispered.

"Look Del, I'll leave you two together. I'll get the lift back up."

Della shook her head and pushed my wheelchair up close to the slab. His skin was rubbery and yellow.

"Just look at him Janie."

I wanted to cut through the insidious melodrama and shout. To yell the obvious. Here was a man who finished himself off out of spite.

Della had called to pick up the hoover, and Fred Hams had made her a cup of coffee, and in monosyllables had tried to persuade Della to "try again". Then, I imagine, Della felt the sweet throb of power and decided to dally with Fred Hams's regret.

"I'm going to the shops," she trilled; "I'll think about it."

Fred Hams clenched his fat fingers and started to cry.

"I'll only be half an hour," crooned Della.

So he planned a suicide scene, and took a few sleeping pills, but didn't reckon on Della having a flash of self-esteem and going to the hairdresser's, or that he, giddy from whisky and mogadon, might fall on the coal scuttle and cut his great fat head open, and bleed to death.

I am devoid of sympathy. It was a waste of a nice perm, that's all.

Della was holding his dead face in her hands and kissing his dead eyes.

"Stop that!" I was afraid his head might fall off and roll into my lap.

That's when she kissed him on the mouth, and his lips curled over his brown teeth and stayed there.

She turned to me sweetly.

"Janie, will you come with me to the funeral?"

The room was so white it felt as if we were standing in the middle of a cloud. It stank of air freshener. Della wore a pink mackintosh and smiled. She reminded me of a house caller for the Salvation Army. I was irritated.

Last August she had left him for the first time and tried to take up yoga, but had to leave the class because he frightened the other peaceable students by throwing bricks at the window. In September he broke her arm . At Christmas he took the one photograph she had of the two of us, dressed in our aunties' ballgowns and high shoes, standing in the back lane with our proud faces, lipstick on our mouths, hair carefully spun into corkscrew ringlets. Fred Hams tore it into pieces, and threw it into the River Tyne. I thought about myself too, her sister, struggling with an inadequate dustpan behind her, trying to clear up the debris, the stains, the broken locks; and this last time, when Della defiantly emerged on my doorstep and said that was the end of her and Fred Hams; and we'd got drunk on cheap sherry, and I said she could live with me if she gave me her hoover.

But the morgue is too holy. I am dumb as a cadaver.

I said I would go to the funeral. I can't refuse Della. She might be demented, but she is my weak, pink sister.

We acted our way through childhood. I was the queen, enthroned in an archaic wheelchair, and she was the princess. She had a broken jewellery box where she kept shells she found on the beach, and trinkets from Christmas crackers, and if I was crying, or aching, or had been verbally savaged by the hard boys, or had been mauled by sentimental girls with Christian attitudes, she would run and get the box and open it, and let me touch her worthless treasures.

"These are the royal jewels," she would whisper. "These are ours."

I believe my sense of worth, my career, and my pragmatism are due to those experiences of believing I was somehow more than ordinary; that I was royal. I went to college. I got a job. I am a television presenter now. I do stuff like birthday greetings and local news. The world sees me from the waist up. Perhaps if Della had been the queen, not just a princess, she wouldn't have met Fred Hams, or lost hold of the thread of who she was.

That night, at my bungalow, we brushed our hair and put on wincyette pyjamas. I made her hot milk and sang "Are You Lonesome Tonight?" then we lay together in my wide double bed and listened to the shipping forecast.

In the morning we got ready for the funeral. Della dreamily dressed me, the way she used to do when no one else was there. Then, quietly, she made herself beautiful. She plaited her long hair, and dabbed perfume on her lacy wrists. She put on a small dark suit, and drew a pearly lipstick across her mouth.

I phoned for a taxi, but the woman on the switchboard was dubious.

"It will be difficult," she snapped. "Especially with a wheel-chair. There's a royal visit on. All the cabs are out."

I told her my name, but in this case it made no difference. The Queen was in town. Railings had been freshly painted. Tramps had been removed from pavements. Bright shrubs had been bunged into civic flower beds. We were forced to walk, Della pushing me past the newsagents and the post office, with pictures of the queen looking resigned from all the newspaper stands.

I felt as if we were playing an imaginary game; acting out some formal ceremony; dressed up, wearing our mothers clothes and singing patriotic hymns in a dirty street. I could feel Della bursting with ritual, glorying in it, transported by the solemnity of the occasion.

I was hoping that once this charade was over we could have a holiday and forget about Fred Hams. I started planning a week in the Hebrides; somewhere with a wind that might blow this gloom away. By then we were gliding through the gates of the cemetery and I could hear canned music and smell the damp pages of hymnals.

It was so quiet. We ambled along a gravel path between some heavy pine trees, turned the corner and found ourselves faced with a cortège of Hamses and close friends of Hamses, with a brutish, familiar-looking man leading the assembled mourners.

"That's her!!" he roared, pointing above me at Della. "That's the bitch that drove my brother to his grave!!"

Simultaneously, as he charged at us, the female members of the family screamed. It was an awful sound; a primitive, terrifying wail. He lurched. I could smell the alcohol on his clothes.

We were good as dead.

"But I loved him!" screamed Della, and collapsed  She lay, like broken china on the ground. I did an instantaneous three point turn, as Fred's brother reached for my neck.

I have never been brave, but I have a strong survival instinct. I dragged Della onto my lap. She was light, like a child.

"It's alright," I shouted. "We're going home now."

His goliath shadow obliterated the faint sun. Then I realised that a dozen screeching women, all over fifty, were clinging to our attacker's badly made suit, and that it wasn't just my forceful words that kept him from beating us into the grit.

I was wheeling backwards, with Della slumped over me, her shoes scraping a track on the path.

I could hear the wails from right outside the cemetery. My arms throbbed. An eighty year-old lady stopped to ask me if I needed some help. Together we put Della down on the pavement and I hailed a cab.

It took a long time for the comatose cab driver to understand the mechanics of the wheelchair. He spoke to me very loudly and slowly. I was sweating and afraid that the black snake of the cortège would pursue us. I pleaded with my purse in my hand.

When we were finally settled on the polythene-covered back seat of the taxi and had waved to our elderly samaritan, I watched Della's eyes flicker open.

"What's going on?" she groaned.

"It just didn't work out," I said practically.

"Is he buried yet?" she whispered.

"I expect so."

We held hands then, and looked out of the window.

The street was lined with people, holding flags and waving.

A brass band was playing its heart out in front of us.

Della sat up, suddenly interested. She started to wave at the crowds, and they cheered and waved back. I laughed.

Della turned to me, excited.

"Look, Janie ! They think I'm the bloody queen!"

And we purred along in the black taxi waving and smiling, while Fred Hams lay dull and cold in the corner of a suburban cemetery.

# Beyond

Beyond the wide motorway that runs hopefully North, blue and green and red with light, that's where I live. All around me cranes hook metal arms like arthritic grandfathers, although since the council painted them pastel colours they are more like grandfathers in new Marks and Spencers polo necks.

My family has always lived here. Sometimes in high flats, sometimes down in the low estates by the river. Up and down, but never out. My mother once told me that our ancestors came from Norway. She said they were Norse warriors, and that was why we must stay in sight of the old North Sea, because we are always waiting for the others to arrive.

My mother was a marvellous liar. It was her lifetime's hobby. If she told the truth it worried her. The truth was lifeless, like a dying tree, that only flowered with blossoming embellishments.

My mother's other hobby was planning to kill my father. When he went out, my sister, my mother and I would sit and talk about breaking his gristly white fingers, rather like surgeons discussing a forthcoming operation. I am not making light of it. He had hands like eagle's claws, bent and mean. He walked like a limping rottweiler. Every door in the place had boot marks etched into it. No cup had a handle. We were at risk, on the border land between motorway and sea, waiting.

When my mother came back from the refuge the third time she was even stronger than before. She'd been going to aerobics and weight-lifting classes, and she was over fifteen stone. When we touched her she felt hard, like concrete under sacking. She had lovely big legs that you could hang on to.

She told us that the refuge was in a big hotel near the station with room service and orchids in vases in the foyer. She said that every night her and the other battered ladies had dances in the ballroom, and that the food was cooked by a Scandinavian called Olga, who put sausages on silver-plated bowls and sang traditional songs in the kitchen. Although this image wasn't much like what they showed on the television, it was infinitely preferable, and we begged her to take us with her next time she went, instead of sending us to granny's.

That time she'd been writing poems about her experiences, which were pinned to my bedroom wall for a while before my father ripped them down. Even then she laughed and said they were only photocopies and the others were lodged with the city archivist. One of the poems was called IF I WAS A CRANE, and another was called OUR DOG. I keep meaning to call into the city archive and check if they are there. You never know.

When my mother was home we had the best meals in the street, thanks to her thieving skills, which she told us she learnt during a short career as a magician's assistant. People were always calling round to sample our stolen meals; cheesecakes and smoked bacon, pizzas with pineapple chunks, bars of Galaxy chocolate and spinach quiche. By the time I was ten I had developed quite a sophisticated palate, which I am now trying to rediscover.

One day my mother appeared with a baseball bat from Bainbridge's. It was a fine, well-crafted bat, and as soon as my sister and I got a chance we ran out into the backyard and started practising shots like American children. My sister put her peaked cap on backwards, and we shouted YEAH! every time one of us hit the dog's ball. Then we broke the kitchen window and my sister peed herself, because father had just come in, and you had to be quiet as a dead dog in that house if you wanted to survive.

When mother came in we were both crying and sitting in a cold bath. My sister had bruises like orange flowers all over her back and although I couldn't see myself my head was jammy and hot and bulging down one side.

When she saw us she sent my father out with a ten pound note. He was so surprised that he went, shaking his fist at us all the way down the stairs, us standing like little ghosts wrapped in towels at the top, just looking, with mother towering behind us in her dangerous red dress, saying sweetly that tea would be ready for seven o' clock.

We listened to his unhealthy footsteps dragging away down the street to the Labour Club, then mother got us dressed quickly, as if it was a war situation and we were refugees. She said we should go to granny's, because a clairvoyant had told her that granny would win the Pools, and the first person she saw would get the best share. Then she gave us a basket of things to take; fags and whisky, and a packet of best French biscuits. Granny lived down by the purple crane and never took off her blue dressing gown. She had two canaries called Frigg and Odin, and a first-aid kit full of eye patches and half curled tubes of noxious ointments. When we got there we spent most of the night on her semi-circular settee rifling through these and watching a film about an unhappy sailor.

So we only found out what happened later, from my mother.

This is what she told us.

My father was in the Labour Club, drinking dreamily with an Irishman called Joey, who was reciting Celtic verse through his long matted beard. I only know this because he came round later and recited some more to us with tears in his eyes, and said how our father loved poetry which was news to me.

My mother took the baseball bat, and splashed some stolen eau-de-cologne on her swollen wrists. She tied her flyaway hair back in a thick pony tail and did some aerobics in the hall, and then walked demurely up to the Labour Club.

She waited in an alley behind the club for my father. Her hands were wide with fear, she said, and her great knees shook, making a terrible noise, like flapping sails. She was sure as hell hoping he'd be on his own when he fell out of the bar and not with Joey, because she'd decided to kill my father, and she preferred not to have to kill two men, although she would if she had to.

At around ten o' clock my father staggered out of the door and began his eerie, steady sway homeward, down the stinking alley. My mother got the baseball bat well in the grip of her big fingers. Then, as he came close, she suddenly thought of a kiss they'd had on a car ferry and something in her big dangerous red heart re-lented; a feeling like Cornish fudge, she said, and she decided to permanently maim him instead.

When she could smell his tarry breath, she stepped out and brought the bat down in a splintering, mighty arc against his knees, and he toppled, screaming with pain.

Then she ran home, poured herself a mug of Tia Maria, and waited.

After over an hour, as she sat in syrupy silence, she heard a moaning from behind the door.

The door scraped open and my father's head drooped, like a mongrel, onto the Welcome mat. Our dog licked him deferentially.

"Sweetheart," said mother from her chair. "What's happened to you?"

"You'd better call an ambulance," he spluttered. "I've been mugged."

"Not robbed I hope?" she said, still sitting there.

"No," he groaned. Then he looked up with narrow, calloused eyes. "I know who it was though."

Mother squeezed the handle of the baseball bat on the floor by the chair.

He wiped his head bravely.

"There were three of them," he looked up woefully at his wife. "And I saw their faces; every one of them."

He fainted.

We writhed with laughter and made her tell us again and again. Those words became engraved on my horizon, as solid and as structured as the high, bent cranes.

After that he shrank, and it wasn't because of his legs that got better rather quicker than anyone had expected. He just lost his height, and his mouth stopped curling at the edges.

Mother, on the other hand, grew at least three inches and had a new smell about her. It was like meatballs. I noticed that when we went out to the shops, people would step to one side when she walked along the pavement, as if she was royalty, and look at her in cafes with admiration. Once I realised it wasn't admiration at all. It was a store detective that had been following her. But other times I'm sure it was.

Another thing that was odd was that for the first time my parents seemed to like each other. It was certainly the best three years of their marriage, that ended when he fell off a bridge into a scabby river, in broad daylight, sober. He had climbed up to show my mother a steel rivet that he had made in nineteen forty-seven when he worked in the construction business. She had wanted to jump in after him, she said, but the shock riveted her to the spot and all she could do was blink. It was my first real experience of death and I was surprised how much we all missed him. After that there was a plethora of deaths. I became quite nervous of heights. Granny died next, and with her went the canaries in sympathy.

Then mother had a heart attack on her way to the fishmonger's; dying dramatically in her red coat, half way across a zebra crossing; causing a traffic jam of lorries filled with frozen cod; leaving my sister and me and a hundred nameless cousins.

Sometimes I envy my sister. She has a clear-headedness that

keeps her feet on the ground. Her shoulders are small and square and she has a noble nose. She washes her hair in vinegar and is good at javelin throwing.

She moved inland; a step that took her away from the murky smells of our childhood. She got a job with a complicated title. She has mother's furniture and I let her keep the baseball bat. She tells me not to idealise our mother and listens to American women singing songs in minor keys. She is not like me.

I am embarrassed by the next part of this story. Social workers and text books will tell you how I sought out my father in my husband. All I can say is, when I met Hughie he could dance very nimbly, and he had very good taste in clothes, and a job as a white collar worker in a prawn factory.

We lived in the highest block of flats, swaying in the cloudy dust of the motorway. Beautiful flats inside; spacious, like tree-houses with wide windows through which all I could see was sky. I put mirrors up, so that when I sat in the centre of the sitting room, sky was everywhere.

Every Friday and Saturday Hughie would go out with his friend Lewis who lived in the flats opposite. Every night when Hughie came home he would push and kick and shout, until I was lost in a giddy circle of black stars.

For a long time there was grit in my heart. My eyes were watery fjords. The trouble was I felt all right as long as I didn't go out. Going out meant becoming aware of how high up I was. I grew to crave the emptiness of sky; the heightlessness of it.

I think I was grieving.

I was certainly mute as marmite. Perhaps that's why he hit me. From the moment I heard Hughie staggering out of the unremitting lift, then walking to the balcony to wave across at Lewis, then walking back to our door, his step hardening as it touched the mat, I was absent, not in my own body. I was somewhere out there in the sky.

This routine went on and on, until, unlike my mother, I grew crooked, like my old granny or a crane. I took to laying things out; hairbrushes, toiletries, kitchen utensils, in patterns on the candlewick bedspread. I found this activity oddly soothing.

As far as I can see change is a coincidental thing, not an act of will. It was a Saturday night when I forgot to leave the door unlocked for Hughie. One of the reasons I forgot was that I was having a vision.

I found myself pressed to the window, looking over the sea. It was a smoky night, yellow and streaky. Smog hung below, so that all the tiny cars and streets were obscured. Fog horns were droning lifelessly in the distance. Then I saw a boat; curved and fluted; a long Viking boat, pulling through the clouds like an angels' raft and my mother was at the helm. She was wearing a great helmet and singing. I waved at her gliding by and caught the shadows of dolphins dipping and swimming in her wake.

I might have opened the window and stepped out, but instead I heard Hughie pushing at the door. His voice was angry, flat and dense, as if he was speaking another language. Then he stopped shouting and I heard him go to the balcony to say his goodbyes to Lewis.

The boat had gone. I ran to the door, opened it , and there was Hughie, hanging over the balcony, swaying and waving. I took a few steps towards him and grabbed the waistband of his trousers. It was like throwing a lifebuoy overboard. He just disappeared into the yellow clouds.

About an hour later the police knocked gently on the door and told me about the terrible accident. I was in shock. They gave me hot sweet tea and phoned my sister.

As I told you before I am trying to rediscover my taste buds. I like strong salty foods and pickles. A crime is on my breath and sometimes I try to cover it up with pungent foods. Last night my sister and I got an Indian take-away and drove up to the light-house on the point. We sat in her car with the radio on and reclined in the soft seats, our fingers red and shiny from the tandoori. I told her everything, and her thin body shook with laughter, and her hair reflected the little twinkling lights from the power station.

"I don't believe a bloody word of it!" she said. "Boats in the sky!"

Then we sat quiet for a while longer, until I said:

"What's wrong with lies?"

And across the old North Sea I could hear mother nodding her head and laughing.

Making the waves roll over the shore.